# Girls From Da Hood 15

# Girls From Da Hood 15

*Treasure Hernandez, Katt*

*and Marcus Weber*

*www.urbanbooks.net*

Urban Books, LLC
300 Farmingdale Road,NY-Route 109
Farmingdale, NY 11735

ISBN 13: 978-1-64556-504-8
EBOOK ISBN: 1-64556-505-X

First Trade Paperback Printing November 2023
Printed in the United States of America

10 9 8 7 6 5 4 3 2 1

*This is a work of fiction. Any references or similarities
to actual events, real people, living or dead, or to real
locales are intended to give the novel a sense of reality.
Any similarity in other names, characters, places, and
incidents is entirely coincidental.*

Distributed by Kensington Publishing Corp.
Submit orders to:
Customer Service
400 Hahn Road
Westminster, MD 21157-4627
Phone: 1-800-733-3000
Fax: 1-800-659-2436

# *Lust*

by

*Treasure Hernandez*

# Chapter 1

"Ouch!" The pained cry of a young woman filled a dark bedroom. "Shit."

Amira James was in the middle of sneaking back into her room on the second floor. She had fallen to the floor with a thud, and she tried to stifle any more noise threatening to come from her lips. Her hip was on fire from the minor fall, but she knew there wasn't much time if someone was coming to check and see what the racket was about. Limping, she stood up and closed the window. She kicked off her shoes and began to tiptoe to her bed, but a light flipping on in the room stopped her in her tracks. Thinking that her hotshot lawyer father caught her red-handed, she feared the worst. However, Amira sighed with relief when she swiveled around and saw who was sitting in the lamp chair.

"Winnie," she said, addressing the family's house-keeper, "you scared me. I thought you were Daddy."

"Mmm, and if I had been, you wouldn't be able to leave this house for weeks," Winnie exclaimed. "You know I had to talk the man out of putting bars on your window."

Winnie had been with the James family since before Amira could walk. She was a beautiful, wide-set woman in her early sixties and more like family than a house-keeper. When Amira was just 5 years old, her mother ran off with the gardener, so Winnie stepped up to help raise her. Amira's father, Aramous James, was one of the most prominent lawyers in Georgia. So that meant he was a busy man. Sometimes too busy to spend time with his daughter. Winnie did all she could to keep her in check, but once Amira turned 18 and graduated high school, she became even more rebellious. In her mind, she was grown and couldn't wait to be off to college out of state. But to Winnie and James, she was just a spoiled girl who had never grown up.

"Even if he did, it's not like it would matter. I'll be gone in a few months anyway," Amira said with a shrug.

She stripped out of the cute pink, two-piece skirt outfit she'd been wearing and tossed it in the hamper inside of her large closet. Next, she grabbed an oversized shirt from her drawer and put it on before climbing into her pink canopy bed. Winnie just shook her head.

"I really wish you would reconsider going away to Florida for college. I almost lost my mind sitting here waiting for you to return to this house. I can't imagine how I will feel when you're somewhere you don't know anybody."

"Winnie, Daddy treats me like I'm a kid. You said it yourself. He wanted to put bars on my window. Who wants to live like that? Plus, I won't be alone. Meka is going to the same college, remember?" Amira said, bringing up her childhood best friend.

"Lord, how could I forget?" Winnie rolled her eyes. "That girl is trouble. And I bet she's the one you were with tonight. Let me guess, some party with cute boys."

"Yes, and I had a ball," Amira said with a grin, but when Winnie cut her eyes at her, she cut it short. "If I would have told Daddy, he wouldn't have let me go."

"And with good reason. You know, with your father's job, he's always worried about you. Especially with this new case."

"Well, nobody told him to defend criminals, did they?"

"You watch your tone with me, girl. I may be 60, but I can still beat you down if I have to." Winnie pointed a finger at her.

"I'm sorry. I just . . . I just want to have a normal life."

"Look around you, girl." Winnie motioned around at the spacious room and expensive décor. "This and that Range Rover you drive comes with a price. Now, if you had friends that enjoyed doing wholesome things, I'm sure your father wouldn't mind you leaving the house. But you want to run around in the bad part of town with hoodrats."

"But—"

"Aht! Hush now, and get some sleep. It's nearly two in the morning. I'll think about letting your father know about this."

She got up and left the room quietly. Amira smiled to herself because she knew Winnie wouldn't tell. She never did. She rolled over on her side and grabbed her phone. The first thing she did was check her social media post from the night. One thing she could say about herself was that she had it going on, from the pretty face to the body bodying the way it was supposed to. The blond skunk stripe in her twenty-two-inch transparent lace wig had set the entire outfit off, and her post was already at 500 likes. Her phone vibrated with a text from Meka.

You made it home, best friend?

Amira responded quickly: Yeah, I did. Winnie caught me, though, but it's cool. She won't tell my dad.

Good. Can you meet for brunch in the morning? Those fine-ass boys we met want to take us for some food.

Amira smiled, remembering the tall, caramel-com-plected sexy thing from the house party. He hadn't said too much to her, but she knew he was feeling her because he was staring from across the room.

Yeah, that's cool. Just send the address.

Amira sent the message and closed her phone. She put it on the charger under her pillow and closed her eyes because all princesses needed their beauty sleep.

# Chapter 2

The next morning, Amira hummed as she moved around her closet, trying to put together the perfect brunch outfit. She didn't know if she wanted to go with a Hilary Banks or a Fran Drescher vibe. Ultimately, she felt she was more of a Fran girl that day. The square-neck orange body con dress accented all of her curves, and the white mule heels made them sit up properly. After brushing out the curls in her hair, Amira put on a white beret and grabbed her white and gold Gucci top handle bag to match. She was very much into fashion, and looking good every day was a must. It didn't matter that she wasn't a model. Being magazine cover-ready made her feel good.

She left her bedroom in the large mansion and went down the hallway to the spiral staircase. She knew that Winnie must have been making breakfast from the smell in the air. Amira had already made up her mind that she would eat at home first. That way, she wouldn't have much appetite at the restaurant. She felt it was unbecoming of a lady to gorge on food in front of boys. But then again, it was also unladylike to scale up the side of a house to climb through a window.

When she made it down the stairs, she went into the kitchen. She found Winnie standing over the stove and her father seated at the dining table. He was scrolling through his phone, no doubt looking at the stock numbers as he did every morning. Like his daughter, he was dressed to impress in a nice-fitted suit. Aramous was in his early forties but looked a decade younger, even with the trickle of gray on his head and beard. Growing up, it used to work Amira's nerves how all her friends had crushes on her "fine" daddy. And she also had to admit that he was quite the lady's man. She'd lost count of how many women had come and gone in his life. Through it all, he remained loyal to only one thing—his work.

"Good morning, Daddy," she said in a singsong voice, kissing his forehead.

"Good morning, baby girl," he replied, not looking up from his phone.

Winnie made Amira's plate and loaded it with French toast, bacon, and eggs. The smell went straight to Amira's nose and made her mouth water. She hurried to sit down and eat. While she dug in, Winnie poured her a glass of orange juice and set it in front of her.

"Where are you headed, beautiful? Paris?" Winnie asked.

"Meka and I are going to hang out."

Upon hearing Meka's name, Aramous finally looked up. Once his eyes fell on his daughter, his brow furrowed.

"And where is Meka dragging you today?"

"We're just going to brunch," Amira told him.

"But you're eating now."

"So? I could be hungry again in an hour."

"There's gonna be boys there, huh?" Aramous shook his head, and Amira smirked. "The last time Meka had you around some boys, they were thugs. You remember what happened?"

"Daddy."

"I know you remember. Tell me the story."

"It's not Meka's fault the guy robbed that gas station. How were we supposed to know he was going to do that?" Amira groaned.

She remembered the horrid night a year before when they'd gotten a ride from some hustler Meka knew. The bad thing was, Aramous had been furious. The good thing was, it was the reason he bought her a Range Rover, so nothing like that could ever happen again. However, he never let it go, and it just added fuel to the fire of his not liking Meka.

"Why can't you make better friends? What about Don's daughter across the street? She seems like a good girl."

"Who, Amanda?" Amira made a face. "Daddy, that white girl is more coked out than the plug."

"At least she comes from good stock. Meka comes from trash."

"If I'm not mistaken, Meka lives in Lakewood Heights. The same neighborhood *you* come from."

"And if you think I did everything I could to make it out for my child to go running back, you're out of your mind." Aramous slammed one of his palms on the table. "That girl is trouble. She's going to lead you down the wrong path."

"I'm not hungry anymore." Amira threw her napkin and silverware on the table. She stood up, and before she could storm out, she glared at her dad. "I see why my mom left."

Once the words were out of her mouth, she rushed out of the kitchen, ignoring her father angrily calling for her to return. She didn't because even if she did, he was out of time for her that morning anyway. It was like any quality time they spent. All he wanted to do was scold her. It was annoying and the reason she couldn't stand being around him, especially when he got to talking about Meka. He hadn't liked her since they were kids. And when he put Amira in a private school, he thought that would end their friendship. However, he hadn't counted on Meka getting a scholarship that paid for her tuition.

Their friendship was the one thing in Amira's life that he seemed unable to control. And that was what it appeared to be about to Amira. The control of it all. It was probably why her mother ran off and abandoned her. She pushed him out of her mind just like she knew he would her when he got in front of his high-profile clients at work.

She let out a loud sigh when she was behind the wheel of her pink vehicle and grabbed a pair of shades from the middle console. Before pulling off, she checked her phone for the address of the brunch spot. It was almost ten o'clock, and that was the time they were supposed to meet up. She put the location in her GPS and let it lead the way. As she drove, her phone kept ringing in her lap, and she kept ignoring it without looking. She knew it wasn't Meka because she had a unique tone as a ringer. Amira assumed it was her dad trying to talk, and she was done talking to him for the day.

When she got to the restaurant, she could see Meka sitting on the gated patio with two handsome men. Amira instantly felt herself grow lighter as a grin came to her face. She parked the Range Rover and sprayed on some perfume before leaving the car. Meka waved to her when she saw her approaching the restaurant. Amira walked inside the busy restaurant, where the host greeted her.

"How many?" he asked.

"My friends are actually outside on the patio waiting for me. Is it okay if I just head out?"

"Of course. Just go down this hallway, and the door leading outside will be on your left," he said, pointing in the direction.

"Thank you."

Amira followed his instructions and found the patio door. She held it open for a woman walking back with a few trays in her hand and then headed out herself. An empty seat next to the caramel-skinned guy from the night before awaited her, and he stood up to pull it out for her.

"Thank you," she said when she sat down.

"Mmmm, we like a gentleman," Meka teased with a wink.

He smiled down at her, and that was when she remembered that his eyes were hazel. Maybe it was the shots of alcohol she'd had because she didn't remember his hair being braided in singles either. Actually, when she thought about it, she didn't even remember his name. He was dressed casually in a flannel shirt and jeans. He gave her a dashing smile and took her in.

"You look amazing," he said in a deep baritone voice, making Amira's stomach fill with butterflies.

"Thank you, so do you," she responded.

"Girl, you really do look fire. That orange is hitting," Meka added.

One thing her girl was going to do was hype her up. But Amira had to give Meka props too. She was sitting very pretty that morning. The sleeveless black top, houndstooth skirt, and black pumps with thigh-high socks were definitely a look. In high school, people used to call them the Barbie Twins because they were always put together. Meka had a very light complexion because her father was Puerto Rican, and all the boys thirsted over her because of her exotic features.

"Thank you, baby. You knew I had to step because I knew you would be here looking all good."

"You know it." Meka giggled and pointed at the guy sitting next to Amira. "So *Tevin* was just telling us about his trip to Malibu a few weeks ago."

*That's his name,* Amira thought. She just knew she would embarrass herself by asking, but Meka came through in the clutch.

"Oh, really? That sounds fun," Amira said, turning to him.

"It was. Me and Pete are planning our next trip. Maybe if we get to know each other better, you can come. If that's cool with you."

"Who's Pete?" Amira asked, confused, and caught Meka shooting her a glance from across the table.

Amira looked and noticed her friend slightly jabbing her head toward the guy sitting next to her and realized that *he* was Pete. She giggled in spite of herself and was happy when the others joined in.

"Damn, were you that lit last night, shawty?" Tevin joked.

"I wouldn't say lit, but I was on my level," she said. "I'm glad you asked us out for brunch, though. I would hate for someone as handsome as you to get away from me so easily."

The two shared a look right before the waitress came to take their orders. Since Amira hadn't finished her breakfast at home, she was hungry. But all she ordered was a muffin and a mimosa. When asked to show her ID, she pulled out the fake ID she'd made. The waitress barely looked at hers or Meka's before nodding and scribbling down their orders. She didn't even bother to check the boys' IDs when they ordered their drinks. When she left, Tevin and Pete excused themselves to the bathroom, leaving Meka and Amira alone. Amira used the time to check her phone, and when she did, she groaned loudly.

"What is it? Your daddy tripping on you again?"

"I thought that's what it was, but no, girl. Somebody was blowing my phone up on the way here, and I figured it was my daddy. Girl, it's Jerron."

"Jerron, as in your crazy-ass ex-boyfriend Jerron?"

"That's the only Jerron I know," Amira said, shaking her head.

She and Jerron had dated most of her senior year of high school. He graduated a year before her, and they seemed like a match made in heaven. He was her first love. He also was the first and only person she'd given herself to sexually. When he graduated, he opted not to go to college. Instead, he made a name for himself in the streets. Things were fine at first, but it soon grew too much for Amira. She didn't want to be with someone who, at any second, could die or go to jail. And when he asked her to stash some of his drugs for him, she knew it was time to break things off. So she did, and he hadn't taken it well.

"Have you seen him since he—"

"No." Amira shook her head.

"Mmm. Girl, I still think you're crazy for not putting him in jail after he put his hands on you. Hell, that's something you should have told your daddy."

"I just wanted it to end after he did that to me. I didn't want to drag it out," Amira said.

She shook the quick flashback of Jerron's hands around her neck out of her head. They'd been outside Meka's house when she told him she wanted to break up. He went berserk.

"You're never gon' leave me, you hear me, bitch?" he'd said.

She could still feel the heat from his breath on her face as he choked the life out of her. She still smelled the stench of alcohol on his breath. He might have killed her if Meka hadn't run out to stop him. She cleared her throat and put her phone away, hoping Jerron would eventually get the point. It was over between them.

Moments later, Tevin and Pete came back to the table. Amira saw that their eyes were way lower than they had been before. She didn't smell any marijuana, but the vape pen sticking out of Tevin's pocket clearly indicated they were high. She didn't see anything wrong with it. Lots of people she knew got high. She was more of an occasional drinker but didn't really fool with drugs.

When the food came, they all dug in. The rest of the morning was filled with laughter and them all getting to know one another better. When it was time to go, Amira was feeling bubbly and cheesy. The two mimosas she drank had her feeling herself. Meka rode there with them but was leaving with her. The guys walked them to the Range Rover, and Tevin raised a brow, impressed.

"Nice whip," he complimented.

"Thanks. It was a gift from my dad."

"He must be rolling in cash, huh?"

"I guess you can say that." Amira shrugged. "He's a lawyer."

"Word? Is that what you'll be studying in Florida? Law?"

"Hell no." Amira turned her nose up. "I want to be a journalist. Maybe start my own magazine."

"Dope," Tevin said, staring at her in wonder. "I guess it's time for me to get out of here. You have my number now. Make sure you use it."

"Okay."

"I'm for real, Amira. I'm trying to keep this vibe rolling."

"Okay," she giggled and hugged him.

*Damn, he smells good,* she thought as she stepped on her tiptoes to bury her nose in his neck.

It felt so good being in his arms that she didn't want to let go, and he felt the same by the reluctant way Tevin stepped back. He slowly backed away and gave an awkward wave before turning away and walking to where he parked his car. Meka was tonguing Pete down in farewell on the other side of the vehicle. When he finally came up for breath, he squeezed her butt before walking away.

"Get your fast ass in the car," Amira joked, pointing to the SUV. "Just fast."

They were laughing as they got into the car. When Tevin drove by, he gave a honk, and Amira waved. She was getting comfortable in her seat when her phone rang again. It was Jerron. Quickly ignoring it, she turned the car on and prepared to reverse out of the parking spot. Right when her foot touched the gas, a black Camaro with darkly tinted windows stopped behind her. She quickly hit the brakes and looked wide-eyed at the car.

"What the fuck is their problem?" she said angrily and hopped out of the car. "Hey, what the hell is wrong with you? You need to move."

She started to walk toward the vehicle, but when the front door opened, and she saw who was driving it, she stopped. It was Jerron. His deep brown face turned up in anger, and she saw the fire in his eyes. She tried to rush and get back into her car, but he was too fast. He caught her before she was able to shut the door.

"Amira!" Meka screamed when she saw Jerron choking her.

"So, this is what the fuck we're doing now? Huh?" Jerron asked through clenched teeth. "You can't answer the phone because you're out with these lame-ass dudes? Bitch, answer me."

Amira couldn't do what he asked because she was too busy gasping for air. The terror coursing through her body was unheard of. He was forcing her to look into his eyes, and all she saw was darkness. Meka had reached over and slapped him, trying to get him to release her, but Amira didn't think he felt the hits. Summoning all her strength, she brought up her knee to hit him between the legs. He cried out and loosened his grip on her enough that she could push him off her. He quickly regained his composure, and when she turned to clamber into the car, he turned her to face him.

"Get off of m—"

Jerron punched her in the eye before she could finish her scream. He pulled his arm back to hit her again, but by then, Meka had found the pepper spray Amira kept in the glove compartment and was spraying him in the face.

"Fuck," he screamed, stumbling back and rubbing his eyes. "Bitch, I'ma kill you!"

"Get in, Amira, get in," Meka urged.

Amira's senses returned to her, and she got in the car. Instead of reversing, she hopped the curb in front of her and sped away from the restaurant. Her hands were shaking as she thought about what had just happened. His words played back in her head. He said he was going to kill her. She didn't understand why he would want to, but she believed him. All she had done was break up with him, but he showed signs of obsession.

"Amira, you *have* to go to the police."

"No." She shook her head. "If I do that, then my dad will know what happened. I can't do that."

"Amira—"

"Just drop it, okay? Let's go to your house so you can put some makeup on my face before I go home."

# Chapter 3

"Good morning, Mr. James. How are you today?"

Aramous had just stepped into his corner office holding a cup of coffee at the firm where he worked. His assistant, Mallory, had come bounding in, wearing her usual skintight dress. That day, she'd opted for green, which looked terrific on her dark skin. She wore her hair extensions. She placed a folder of paperwork in her hands on his desk as he sat.

"Same old, same old," he said with a sigh.

"Another fight with Amira?" she asked knowingly.

"How'd you guess?"

"That," she said, pointing at the coffee in his hand. "The girl drives you straight to the caffeine."

"I guess I have a tell then," he said with a chuckle.

"You have many I've discovered these last five years working for you."

"And what are they?"

"Ha. You think I'd tell you so you can catch yourself? No, sir," Mallory said with a wink. She pointed at the files she'd placed on his desk. "Those are the new developments with the Hinton case."

"New developments?" Aramous asked, picking up the folder. "Please don't say it's bad news. We have everything needed to knock this case out of the park."

"I think the word you're looking for is *had*. You didn't watch the news last night?"

"No, what happened on the news?"

"Your client has been very busy, that's what. They busted another dope house, and now the prosecution has someone willing to testify against your client. You remember Cheryl Pond?"

"Of course I do. That case was all over the news. She was smuggling drugs in from overseas and got caught."

"Yeah, well, in exchange for a lighter sentence, she's ready to testify against her business partner."

"Yeah? And who might that be?"

"Kaleef Hinton," Mallory said, tapping a finger on the folder, "a.k.a. your client."

"No fucking way." Aramous's eyes widened as he sifted through the contents of the folder. "Pictures of them together. Money from his account going into hers. Shit. How the hell does he expect us to fight this?"

"I don't know. I'm just happy that the detective you have on the inside was able to give you a heads-up."

"Me too." Aramous sighed and dropped the folder on the desk. "And what did I tell you about reading through my case files?"

"You knew I was nosy when you hired me," she said with a wink and reached the door.

"Mallory."

"Yes, Mr. James?" She stopped in the doorway to look over her shoulder.

"Why don't you let me take you out for dinner sometime? My treat."

She smirked at the advance. "Mr. James, how often do I have to tell you I don't shit where I lie? We make a good team. I don't want to be one of your play things."

With that, she shut the door to his office, leaving him alone. It wasn't the first time she'd shot him down, but something about her made him not give up. It could have been that she was so attractive to him, or it could have been that even though she wouldn't date him, she treated him well. He would have his day someday, but that day wasn't it, which was fine due to the new challenge he had at hand.

Aramous was a defense attorney who was very good at his job. Most wondered how he could do a job like his since he represented people who most felt were criminals. However, to him, everybody was guilty of something. Having tainted men judge tainted men never sat right with him. Court was nothing but a chessboard. Whoever had the best moves won. It was that simple to him, and he was very good at playing the game.

His latest client was Kaleef Hinton. His kingpin status was no secret in the community. However, it was something that could never be proven. He'd recently gotten caught up in a murder case, but the star witness was found dead in his bathtub, an apparent suicide. The trial would be a walk in the park—or it should have been. With this new information coming to light, Aramous would have to get down to the bottom of it. He needed to figure out exactly what kind of dealings Cheryl had with his client and why she was so eager to rat him out. As with any dangerous client, Aramous knew the risks he ran if he didn't help Kaleef beat the case. They were risks he wasn't willing to take.

# Chapter 4

Amira sat in front of her vanity, staring into the mirror in disbelief. When she got home, she managed to sneak past Winnie to get to her bedroom. She was glad because there was a dark bruise on her cheek. Her lip was swollen, and her face had a few scratches. Seeing the damage Jerron had done made her think that maybe she should have taken Meka's advice and called the police. He was crazy and clearly not taking the hint that she was done with him.

Hours spent sitting in front of the vanity passed, and she didn't know how many calls she ignored. Tears rolled continuously down her face until she finally wiped them away to attempt to cover the damage. The concealer and foundation could only do so much, but soon, she could look at her face without wanting to cry. She sighed, grabbed her phone, and saw that one of the missed calls was from her dad. There was no way that she could tell him what had happened. All he would do was blame Meka. She checked the clock and saw more time than she thought had passed. Her dad would be home any minute. Not wanting to face him, she grabbed her phone and purse to leave.

After she left her room, the goal was to make it to the front door without being detected. However, luck wasn't on her side that time, and she couldn't slip under Winnie's nose. The older woman entered the foyer and stood between Amira and the door.

"And where are you off to so fast?" Winnie asked.

"Just out," Amira answered, not looking her in the eyes.

"You were just 'out.' Where are you going again so soon?"

"Just to hang out with Meka."

It wasn't entirely a lie. Amira didn't know where she was going. But seeing Meka again that day might have been in the cards. She tried to step past, but Winnie grabbed her chin. Amira could tell the older woman was trying to get a closer look at her face. The makeup covered the damage pretty well, but not if someone was as close to her as Winnie was, so she pulled away.

"Tell my dad don't wait up. I'll be home late."

She rushed out the door before she could be stopped again and made a beeline for her vehicle. Once inside, she started it and pulled away from the house. With no destination, she pulled out her phone and sent a message to Tevin, asking where he was. As she drove, she waited for his response and was happy when he called her.

"Hello?" she answered.

"Yo, I didn't think I would be hearing from you this soon. I ain't complaining, though. You good?"

"Actually . . . no," she breathed.

She didn't know why, but something told her to tell him what had happened, even though she was sure he wouldn't want anything to do with her afterward. Who wanted a girl with a diabolical ex?

"What's wrong, shawty? Talk to me. Where you at right now? Pull up to the crib."

"Okay. Send the addy."

"Say less."

She disconnected the call, and seconds later, Tevin texted her with his location. After putting the address in her GPS, she saw that Tevin was in an apartment near her. Usually, she wasn't so quick to pull up on a guy, but she was in a vulnerable state and just needed some comforting energy. It didn't take her long to get to the gated complex. She was just about to call him to come to the gate, but when she looked at their thread, she saw that he'd already sent her the gate code.

She said out loud, "Two-seven-eight-five," as she reached out her window and pressed in the numbers.

The gates opened instantly, and she drove through them toward building E. She parked, and when she got out of the car, she saw Tevin bounding down a set of stairs to greet her.

"Damn, did you speed over here?" He grinned.

"No, I was in the area. I wasn't that thirsty to see you," she teased.

He opened his arms to hug her once he reached her, but he stopped her when she leaned in to give him one. He placed his hands on her shoulders to hold her steady while he looked at her face.

"What happened?" he asked.

"I don't know what you're talking about," she said, looking away.

"Yeah, right. That makeup can't hide that your face is clearly swollen, and it looks like you have a bruise. You ain't look like this at brunch, so what happened?"

Amira shrugged, still not looking him in the eyes. Although she had come over there to talk, she didn't realize how hard it would be to spit out the words. Tevin gripped her chin and forced her to look at him. After a moment, he took her hand and led her to his apartment.

Inside, he had the AC blasting, so it was cool there, and the sweet aroma of vanilla hit Amira's nostrils. His place was set up nicely. There was a large U-shaped gray sectional in the living room with a matching ottoman for them to sit on. She looked around at the abstract paintings he had on his wall. They complemented the blue rug in front of the sectional and the silver wall décor. She also noticed that he didn't have a television in the living room, but what was interesting was that he had beautiful plants all over. Everything was neat and put in the right place, and the carpet even had the vacuum lines she loved so much. Tevin went to the kitchen and grabbed her a water bottle. When he returned and handed it to her, she raised a brow.

"Where is she?" she asked.

"What do you mean?" Tevin looked genuinely confused.

"You obviously have a girlfriend. Where is she? I'm sure she won't be too happy that you have me all in your crib."

"You're funny as fuck," he told her with a laugh. "There is no *she*. This is my shit. I live alone."

"Mmmm," Amira said, not believing him. "This place is too nice and neat. There has to be a bitch somewhere."

"Nah, shawty. My grandma taught me early on that a nasty man was worthless," he said, still laughing. "She also told me that if I want a woman to add to me, I need to be able to add to her on her worst days. Plus, I'm just a clean-ass nigga, and I like nice shit."

"I hear you," Amira said, still not entirely sold.

"But enough about me. Tell me what happened to your face. You got into a scuffle or something?"

"I guess you can say that."

"Damn, that fast?"

"It wasn't any girls. It was . . . It was my ex-boyfriend. He must have followed me to brunch and saw us. It pissed him off, and he did this." She pointed to her face. "I thought I had done a good job of covering it, but I guess not."

"That nigga is a bitch," Tevin said, sitting up straighter. Amira could tell that he was genuinely bothered by the new information. "I can't stand a motherfucka that puts his hands on a female."

"I broke up with him, but he's just not getting the picture. I never thought Jerron would do anything like this to me."

"Wait." Tevin made a face like he was trying to ensure he'd heard her correctly. "Did you just say *Jerron*, as in black-ass Jerron? He push a Camaro?"

"Yeah." Amira furrowed her brow. "You know him?"

Tevin sighed and leaned back on the couch. He brought his hands to his face and wiped down in a stressed motion. When he looked back at her, she saw regret in his expression.

"Yeah, I know that nigga. He works for my older cousin Kaleef. This is all my fault."

"How could this be your fault, Tevin? You didn't know he would put his hands on me."

"Nah. I didn't even know he was involved with anybody the way he keeps bitches on rotation. But it is my fault. I'm the one who invited him to brunch earlier."

"You *what?*" Amira's eyes grew big like saucers.

"I'm sorry, I didn't know. My cousin put me in touch with him awhile back. I didn't know y'all had anything going on. But trust, he will get dealt with for this shit. You're too beautiful for anybody to fuck with your face like that."

He reached out and cupped her cheek tenderly. Although it was a soft touch, her face was so sore that she still winced. The intensity of his gaze made her look down in an embarrassed fashion.

"Stop doing that," he instructed, making her look back at him again.

"Why are you looking at me like that? Like you care? You met me last night at a party, and we barely talked."

"Divine intervention. There's a reason why we were led to this very moment, and I think it's because you need a nigga like me in your life."

"Oh, really?"

"Hell yeah. Everybody does," he joked with a grin.

Something about his smile lit a fire in Amira's chest and between her legs. There was no denying their attraction, but she felt it wasn't the right time to act on it. It was just how he stared at her in that fragile state that did it for her. Like she was still the most beautiful girl in the world. That look alone gave her the courage to scoot closer to him.

"I do," she said.

"Huh?"

"I . . . I do need you. Right now." She slowly moved her hands up the front of his T-shirt, stopping at his chest.

"What you need me to do?" he asked in a lower tone.

"Make me feel good," she breathed before leaning in for a kiss.

Their lips met, and it was the sweetest thing Amira had ever tasted. Their tongues swam in the depths of each other's mouths, and their arms naturally wrapped around each other. Amira wasn't an easy girl, but right then, she wanted . . . no, she *needed* something to make her feel precious again. She knew Tevin didn't love her, but that didn't mean their bodies couldn't pretend like it. She mounted him, and he hiked up her dress, palming her cheeks. She grinded on his large erection and moaned in his mouth. Her hands fumbled with the zipper on his pants, but he stopped her right when she got it down.

"Wait, wait. This ain't right." He shook his head, trying to catch his breath.

"But I want it," she said, trying again to get his pants down.

"Stop," he told her, grabbing her hands. "You're vulnerable right now. I don't want you to feel like I don't want you. I do. One day I do want to dig deep into that pussy, but right now, it just ain't the time. But,"—he kissed her quickly—"I can do something else for you."

"And what's that?"

He grinned mischievously at her, put her down on her back, and spread her legs open. Moving her panties to the side, he bit his bottom lip as he stared at her glistening kitty cat. Softly, he kissed her clit, and she shivered.

"I want to make you feel good. I'm not the kind of nigga you have to do shit for for me to want to see you happy."

His words rang in her ears before he dove in headfirst and devoured her like the Last Supper. Her legs trembled as Tevin went to town. His tongue did things to her that a dick never could. Her hands held on to the back of his head for dear life as he licked and slurped away. When she finally came, she felt her juices sliding down the crack of her butt, and he also licked those up. His moans were what turned her on the most. It turned him on to turn her on. The first orgasm took much of her energy, but that didn't stop her from opening her legs wider so he could keep eating.

"Tevin," she cried out.

"Tell me you love how I eat this pussy," he growled at her.

"Oh, Tevin, I love it. You eat this pussy so good."

"I know. This is what you need. Pretty-ass pussy."

"Tevin . . ."

Her vaginal walls were so hungry and wanted to be penetrated, but he didn't. Not even with his finger. He focused all his attention on her clit, bringing another orgasm quickly after the first. After licking all the excess secretions, he kissed her pussy one last time before getting off the couch and scooping her into his arms. He carried her to the master bedroom and placed her softly on the bed.

Amira was so weak from the tongue-lashing he'd just given her. She couldn't do anything but just stare at him in wonder. Tevin went to the bathroom to wash his face, but when he returned, he climbed into bed with her. She felt . . . safe. He held her, and she snuggled up close to him.

"I guess now we should get to know each other for real, huh?" she joked in a whisper, and he kissed her forehead.

"After I handle Jerron, we'll have all the time in the world for that. Go to sleep."

# Chapter 5

A few days had passed since Tevin's run-in with Amira, and he couldn't explain her hold on his attention. He was infatuated with her. It could have been because they were from two completely different necks of the woods. He could tell that she was a daddy's girl, spoiled, and probably got everything she wanted. On the other hand, he had to climb and scrape for everything he had. If it weren't for his cousin Kaleef putting him on in the drug game after his parents died, he didn't know where he would be. He had enough paper to live flashier than he did, but Tevin enjoyed flying under the radar. A regular crib and a Chevy Impala were good enough for him. He didn't need to showboat his money, but his accounts were hefty.

He liked Amira because she knew nothing about that side of his life but still showed interest. It didn't matter to her; it pleased him that she was impressed by the little he showed her. When he was a boy, his grandmother taught him that if he paid attention close enough, a person would tell him exactly who they were the moment he met them. They wouldn't even have to say a word. And he knew already that she was cool peoples, someone he wanted to pursue. It had taken everything in him not to take her to pound town when she came to his place, but seeing her in such a fragile state had made him want to cater to her needs.

What Jerron had done to her infuriated him, mainly because Tevin was the one who dropped the location. If he hadn't done that, Jerron wouldn't have been able to find Amira to hurt her. And that was why he had to handle it. Not only that, but when he and Pete had gone to the restroom at the restaurant, Tevin had called Jerron, asking him where he was.

"I'm not gonna be able to make it. Maybe next time," Jerron had said.

Tevin knew then that he had been lying. He'd been lying in wait for Amira to be vulnerable. They'd been sitting on the patio, so Tevin was sure Jerron had seen her with him when he pulled in. That probably infuriated him.

It was night when Tevin got to one of the many houses Kaleef had around Atlanta. He parked his car and got out, instantly spotting the Camaro parked on the street. He approached the front door, and the moment he did, it swung open. Anybody in Kaleef's crew knew who he was and gave him the respect he deserved. Not just because he was Kaleef's cousin but because he was lethal. Tevin was young, but he wasn't the one to cross. His exterior might have been that of a chill young cat, but he had the heart of a killer. The two men standing behind the front door nodded at him as he entered. Both men were strapped with pistols and ready just in case someone who wasn't supposed to be there showed up.

Tevin moved past them and bounded up the stairs. The air was cloudy and smelled like the best weed in the city. He could hear loud talking and laughing coming from the kitchen. When he arrived, he saw everybody seated around the kitchen table, Jerron included. Kaleef sat at the head of it, counting a huge stack of money. When he was done, he put a rubber band around it and tossed it to the middle of the table where a brick of cocaine lay.

"Hey, Tev," a topless woman said as she walked by Tevin to join her other half-naked friends in the living room.

It wasn't abnormal for Tevin to see naked women around. He'd become desensitized to it. They were there to count the money, test the product, and suck any of the crew's dicks when the men wanted. Tevin pushed her hand away as she went to rub his stomach.

"Watch out; you probably haven't even washed them shits," he said, turning his nose up at her.

She tooted her nose up at him and rolled her neck as she walked off, clearly upset. He didn't pay her any mind and entered the kitchen. Kaleef smiled big when he spotted Tevin.

"Well, if it isn't little cuz," his voice boomed. Tevin ignored everyone else and walked up to Kaleef, shaking his hand. "Did you handle that drop for me like I asked?"

"You have to ask?" Tevin gave Kaleef a knowing look.

"You? Never." Kaleef grinned. He was much older than Tevin but didn't look like it, especially since the two dressed similarly in style. "I'm just tryin'a tighten up. You know I got this case going on. I don't need any fuckups."

"I hear you, but you know ain't nothing bad coming at you from this way."

"That's what I like to hear. Now, come sit. I want you to hear my latest business venture," Kaleef said, placing a hand on his back and leading him to a seat at the table.

Tevin sat next to Kaleef between him and his right-hand man, Sparrow. Across from him was Jerron, who gave a head nod. Tevin couldn't bring himself to give one back, and that made Jerron smirk. It wasn't the time or the place to check him for what he had done to Amira, but soon, it was something that had to be done. Just looking at Jerron put a bad taste in his mouth.

To be truthful, Tevin wasn't too fond of anyone in Kaleef's crew, Sparrow included. They were all knuckle-heads, and he didn't trust them. They reminded him of vultures, just circling and waiting to swoop in on the next dead body.

"So, what's this business venture you want to talk about?" Tevin asked Kaleef.

"Cuz, what's the one thing that sells at the same magnitude as drugs?"

"I don't know, probably sex."

"Exactly." Kaleef grinned. "The need for sex has this world in a chokehold. Mix in a little high, or a big one, and that need triples."

"So what, you tryin'a run some sort of human trafficking business? I'm not with that."

"Pussy," Jerron threw out, and Tevin's eyes cut in his direction.

"The only thing pussy is men who put their hands on females," Tevin said evenly.

"What I do with my bitch is none of your concern, understand?"

"What I *understand* is that she'd been done with you. *That's* why you put your hands on her. Well, that's what she told me when she was at *my* crib."

Tevin could see that his words had gotten under Jerron's skin. It was his turn to smirk, which seemed to make Jerron even madder. He stood up with clenched fists. Tevin stood up too, ready for whatever.

"Aye, y'all need to chill the fuck out. Sit y'all young asses down up in this motherfucka fighting over pussy. Put your dicks away," Kaleef warned. They glared at each other for a moment before they heeded the warning and sat down. When they did, Kaleef continued speaking. "Nah, I'm not talking about human trafficking. This is something on a larger scale. I'm talking about a place where a person's wildest dreams can come true. All willing participants. Men and women."

"So, a sex club?"

"I guess you could call it that. But I'd like to call it . . . Tranquility."

Tevin thought about it for a few moments. It honestly didn't sound like a bad idea, especially in the era they were in. Sex had gone from being a sacred exchange to being as common as a handshake. He could also see it being a great way to expand their already booming drug market to newer crowds. However, there was one small problem.

"You sure this is a smart thing to do, considering your case?"

"This motherfucka is always a Debbie Downer, Leef!" Sparrow groaned loudly. "Damn, li'l cuz, this is a good business venture. Be happy we're bringing you on the ride."

"One, I'm not your li'l cuz. Two, *we* aren't doing shit for me. The last time I checked, *Kaleef* ran things around here."

"He's right, Sparrow. Chill, man. You're always on my cousin's nuts for some shit. He's the only one at this table asking the right questions."

"It just sounds like hating to me." Sparrow shrugged. "Your case ain't got shit to do with you opening a legitimate business. Plus, he has the best lawyer that money can buy in Georgia."

"That's where you're wrong," Tevin said as his mind calculated the issues with Kaleef's new business plan. "His case isn't anything to take lightly. He has the Feds on his ass, watching his every move. I'm sure they know all of us by name and affiliation. If he opens a new business, they will be all over that too. Undercovers would be all through that bitch waiting to catch us slipping."

"And this is why you have a seat at my table, li'l cuz." When Kaleef nodded in a satisfied notion, the look of annoyance on Sparrow's face shone like a bright light. "You're absolutely right about everything you just said. We have to be smart about this shit, and that's why the business couldn't be in my name. I put it in Grandma's name, her maiden name, until all this shit blows over. So I'm trusting you and Sparrow to run things and make sure my money is right."

"Man, I can do that shit by myself," Sparrow told him.

"But I said both of you," Kaleef snapped.

"Wait, you said you *put* it in Grandma's name. You mean it's already open?"

"Yup," Kaleef said with a big smile. "The place is booming already too. Tranquility has people lining up to get inside and get their rocks off."

Tevin nodded his head as his thoughts took hold of him. Kaleef was a great and calculating businessman, but he often made decisions first and dealt with the blowback later. It usually worked in his favor, but his federal case proved that even he wasn't foolproof. While the others spoke in celebration of the new money venture, Tevin thought only of the business side of things. If he was to be in charge of things there alongside Sparrow, he wanted to be sure that everything was everything. Of course, he knew the dangers that came with his line of work, and that was why he wanted to take every precaution necessary to prevent himself from being in Kaleef's position.

"Leef," he spoke loudly so that he could be heard.

"I know that look," Kaleef said, eyeing Tevin's expression. "What's wrong? You don't think Tranquility is a good idea?"

"Nah, the opposite. You know I love money, especially when it comes smoothly to my pockets. I just thought we should have some membership guidelines in place for this shit to work. People can come and indulge, but only members can buy drugs from us in the club. That way, we don't risk accidentally selling to the Feds."

"Good. Yeah, that's good." Kaleef nodded.

"And no underage girls," Tevin said, looking around the table. "Twenty-one and up. I don't care if her birthday is in one week. We don't need a scandal on our hands. Lastly, you all have high-profile customers that you sell to. Let them know about Tranquility. We can come up with some sort of perks for them if their friends get a membership." When he finished talking, he looked at Sparrow with triumph.

Kaleef patted Tevin's shoulder hard but happily. The grin on his face had gotten wider and turned into a full-on laugh.

"And this is why my legacy will go to you when I'm gone."

# Chapter 6

*Knock, Knock.*

Days had passed since Aramous found out about Cheryl Pond. He had tried everything in his power to get ahead of it and maybe talk her into reconsidering, but he couldn't get close enough to talk. And now that *she* was the star witness, he didn't want to be charged with witness tampering. Aramous knew Kaleef wasn't the kind of man an average person wanted to piss off. However, the mess he was in was of his own doing. Still, telling him the news wouldn't be a walk in the park. When Aramous heard the knock on his office door, he saw Kaleef standing there with two of his henchmen. All were wearing suits and looked like regular businessmen.

"Well, if it isn't my favorite lawyer," Kaleef said, stepping inside the office.

"Kaleef. Sit down. We have some things we need to discuss." Aramous used a pen to motion toward the chair across from his desk.

Kaleef's henchmen stood on either side of him when he sat. Kaleef had the same smug expression on his face that he always had. He thought he was a made man.

"I was a little confused when you asked to see me today, Aramous. I thought the case was closed, especially after Benzino's . . . accident. He was the star witness—hell, the *only* witness. So what's good, man? You need me to sign some paperwork or something?"

"No, actually"—Aramous sighed as he tapped the pen on his desk—"actually, we have a problem. A big problem. The case isn't closed, and they're looking to hit you hard. By the end of the week, they're planning to indict you on a RICO."

"What the *fuck* did you just say to me? How did this go from a murder charge to a goddamn RICO?"

"Does the name Cheryl Pond ring a bell?" Aramous asked, watching the smug expression drop from Kaleef's face.

"That bitch. I knew I should have killed her ass when I had the chance."

"I'm going to act like I didn't just hear that." Aramous shook his head and put the pen down. "Look, man, this is serious. The prosecution believes they already have a pretty solid case, and by locking you up, it will give them more time to build on it. With what she's giving them, plus when your people get to talking—"

"I don't have snitches in my camp," Kaleef snarled, but Aramous gave him a knowing look.

"Once they start getting picked up and slapped with twenty-five to life, you sure about that?"

He'd seen the best of friends turn on each other and organizations crumble. At the end of the day, it was rare for someone to throw their life away to save another, even if it was the person who had been lacing their pockets with money, because freedom was priceless. Kaleef tried to look sure of himself, but the doubt shone through like a beam. Aramous had been in his line of work for a long time.

"Well, you're my lawyer, and I'm paying you good money. What the fuck are we going to do about this?"

"What does Cheryl have on you? It says here that she was your business partner. I assume that means in your illegal dealings?"

"Yes. She was my supplier for a while. Her family is very well connected. I can't believe that bitch turned snitch. Her going to prison has nothing to do with me. She got caught up delivering to some asshole in Florida."

"Well, that's neither here nor there. She's using you as her get-out-of-jail-free card. Does she have anything tangible that can tie you to her smuggling?"

"I don't know. I trusted her. So . . ."

"You might have let your guard down."

"Exactly."

"Okay. I need to get ahead of this. It might be hard with her in protective custody, but a few people in high places owe me favors. Stay off the radar. If they haven't indicted you yet, it's because they don't have everything they need. Let me do my job."

"Yeah, you do that. I don't think I need to remind you of what happens to people who let me down," Kaleef said in a menacing tone.

It was meant to scare Aramous, he was sure. And had he been anyone else, it probably would have. But instead of shaking in his boots, he smiled at his client.

"I don't take lightly to threats, Kaleef. Especially when the pile of shit we're stinking in is of your own making. So, as I said, let me do my fucking job, and you stay off the radar. That kingpin shit might work in the streets, but *I'm* the king in this office. You need me—not the other way around; don't forget it. Now, have a nice day. I'll let you know when I have news."

By how Kaleef's vein in his right temple protruded, he was furious. However, nothing Aramous said was fiction. Kaleef had no one to blame for his ailing luck but himself. He stood up and left the office without another word.

When he was alone in his office again, Aramous sighed. Being a defense attorney wasn't all it was cracked up to be sometimes. Yes, it was lucrative, but it was also a dangerous job. Especially since he had been bold enough to take on a criminal like Kaleef. He planned on doing everything he could to ensure the man walked. Because if he didn't . . . Aramous's life would for sure be in jeopardy.

# Chapter 7

"Tell me!"

Amira's whiny voice filled Tevin's car, and he laughed her off. They'd been dating for a few weeks, and he still felt it was prudent to keep things exciting between them. It drove Amira crazy that he wouldn't tell her where they were going that night. She was dressed sexily in a black top, skirt, and heels. She took significant time on her hair and makeup, hoping she wasn't overdressed for what he had in store. She had a love-hate relationship with his surprises. She loved them because it made her feel special to know that Tevin had thought deeply enough about her. She hated them because being patient was not a strong suit of hers.

"You'll see when we get there, shawty. Be cool."

His voice was calm and even. She turned her head and surveyed him with her eyes. He was fine as hell in his Gucci shirt and gold Cuban link chain. The cologne he wore was making love to her nose. There was nowhere else she would rather be than with him that Friday night, and that was the only reason she decided to "be cool."

She had truly been enjoying her time with Tevin. He was like a breath of fresh air in comparison to Jerron. She didn't have to hide behind a popular girl image with him. She was able to be herself. And she was glad because she learned that they had similar interests. Both loved anime and science fiction. Their favorite food was pasta, and their favorite comedian was Eddie Murphy. They'd already rewatched *Norbit* five times and cracked up each time. She had never been one to believe in fairy tales, but she was falling for him hard and fast. The strangest part was that she knew he would catch her.

A big smile came to her face when they pulled into the parking lot of Bella Italia, one of her favorite Italian restaurants. Their shrimp alfredo was her favorite, and she could already taste it on her tongue. However, right when they were about to get out of the car, Tevin's phone rang, and he answered it.

"What's good, Sparrow?"

Amira tried not to make it too apparent that she was tuned into his conversation. The closer she got to him, the more curious she became. Although Tevin wasn't as flashy as Jerron, he had a lot of money. She knew Jerron was a drug dealer, so when she put two and two together, she figured Tevin was one too. Especially since he and Jerron knew each other. Kaleef Hinton was Tevin's cousin, so she wondered how deep in Tevin was.

"Right now?" he said and then nodded his head. "A'ight, I'm a little preoccupied, but I'ma come through. Yup."

He hung up the phone and instantly looked at Amira with apologetic eyes.

"What?" she asked.

"That was my people. Can we reschedule our date tonight?"

"But why?" she whined. "We're already here."

"I know, baby. But business is business. I have to go handle some things at the club and—"

"I like clubs." She interrupted him and gave him puppy eyes.

"Baby," he sighed. "This isn't a club I want you at, for real. It's one of Kaleef's underground spots that he has me running."

"Well then, that makes you the boss, right? And if I'm with the boss, I'm good."

She gave him a mischievous smile and saw his thoughts churning. Amira hated hearing the word no, and it wouldn't change that night. He might not have known it, but he wasn't going anywhere without her. She didn't want to go back home any time soon. Ever since something happened in her dad's case, he had been on edge and much snappier than usual lately. She would rather be out and about with Tevin doing something—anything.

"Fine." He finally gave in. "But whatever you hear and see has to stay between us, understand?"

"Yes."

"For real. Don't go telling your girl Meka shit."

"I can't tell Meka?" she asked, and he gave her a serious look. "Fine. I won't tell Meka shit."

"Good. The club isn't far from here."

"Do they at least have food?" She heard herself asking as they left the restaurant parking lot.

They drove down a strip toward a booming nightclub a little while later. The word "Tranquility" hung in bold neon lights at the top front of it. A line had formed outside the double doors, but Tevin still pulled right to the front. He motioned for her to get out, and she did.

"What's good, Tev?" one of the big, Black, burly doormen greeted him.

"Shit, Jay. Just checking the spot out real quick. Can you park the whip?" Tevin asked and tossed his keys to the man.

"Fa sho," Jay said, catching the keys and laughing. "Aye, when you gon' upgrade and get you some new wheels? I thought you would have been upgraded to a Benz or some shit by now."

"I'll get a Benz when you get your baby mama back," Tevin shot back, and the other men at the door laughed.

"Aye, fuck you, little motherfucka," Jay said, laughing too. "You'll feel my pain when that fine thing with you leaves your ass just like Ronetta left me."

"I don't plan on going anywhere," Amira said, taking Tevin's hand.

"Yeah, Ronetta said that to me. Now she's fucking her neighbor's broke ass," Jay said, shaking his head. "Anyways, Tev, Sparrow is in there waiting for you."

"Got it. Come on, baby."

Tevin led Amira into the club. The hallway was long, and there was a burgundy curtain at the end of it. Tevin moved it out of the way so that they could keep walking. It was hot, loud, and crowded. The lights were dim, and a bar stood in the middle of the floor. The DJ had everyone moving their bodies to the beat, and many people bumped into Amira as they made their way through them. Tevin gripped her hand tightly until they reached an exclusive VIP section. Sitting there, a woman in a skimpy outfit on his lap, was a man. He looked to be around Amira's father's age, but he was handsome. The long hair on his head was sandy brown, as was the beard on his chin. When Tevin approached, they shook hands.

"What's good, Tev?" Sparrow asked.

"You know what's good, Sparrow. You called me here."

"Damn, straight to business, no pleasantries?" Sparrow tried to joke.

Amira could tell that Tevin's lighthearted fun with Jay wasn't about to happen with Sparrow. In fact, she noticed that he'd grown a little stiff in Sparrow's presence. His entire body language showed he wasn't fond of the man sitting on the VIP couch.

"Fine, let's get to business then." Sparrow shrugged and then looked at Amira. His eyes trailed her up and down. "Who's this?"

"Somebody who's with me. She's good."

"You sure?"

"Yeah, she wouldn't be here if she wasn't."

"A'ight. Just making sure I can speak freely. You see that motherfucka at the bar?" Sparrow asked and pointed.

Amira followed his finger and saw a white gentleman standing there surrounded by sexy women. They were all over him . . . literally. Their hands caressed any part of his body they could touch, and Amira could tell that one had her hand down his pants. His eyes were rolling to the back of his head, and he was obviously getting his dick jacked off right there at the bar.

"Isn't that Barry Lanes? The politician?"

"That's him, all right. The bastard hasn't paid his membership fee but has been partaking in all the perks."

"You called me down here to check one motherfucka?" Tevin asked, clearly annoyed.

"I figured since it was your idea to have memberships, it should be your idea to patrol them."

Tevin turned back to Sparrow and glared down at him. Sparrow had a complacent look, and Amira felt Tevin's annoyance transfer to her. Tevin might have been young, but he was the wisest person she'd ever met. She didn't like that Sparrow was clearly trying to "little boy" him.

"If something Kaleef approves is put in place, it's all of our jobs to make sure everything is everything, but you know that," Tevin growled. "You might be my cousin's friend, but blood will always be thicker; know that. With that being said, *we* are going to go over there and handle this shit, and then *we* are going to go to the back and discuss business. Get your old ass the fuck up, and let's go."

Tevin's voice was demanding, and there was nothing else to do but to listen. Sparrow hesitated but eventually pushed the girl off his lap and got up. Tevin guided Amira to sit down across from her.

"I'll be back, baby. Order whatever you want off the menu."

"Okay."

She watched the two men walk off. She wanted to see what would happen, but the crowd had thickened, and soon, she couldn't see them. She sighed and grabbed a menu on the table.

"Your man is *fine*," the woman across from her said. "Do you share?"

Her question caught Amira off guard while trying to figure out what flavor wings she wanted. She looked up at the woman and took in her appearance for the first time. She was pretty, but she would be prettier without the three nose piercings she had. Her black lipstick matched her leather getup, and her hair was cut pixie style. She licked her lips at Amira, and Amira made a face.

"Excuse me?"

"I asked if you like to share his dick. I would love to let him fuck me while I eat your pussy. You look like you taste like . . . peaches."

"Bitch, what the fuck kind of shit are you into?" Amira asked, and the woman looked offended.

"Umm . . . obviously the same kind of shit you are if you're here."

"What is that supposed to mean?"

"Look around you. What do you think I mean?"

She waved her hand around, and slowly, Amira turned around. She hadn't really paid attention to anything when she first came in, but that time she did. She saw what she had seen at first glance, people dancing. But when she looked closer, she noticed men and women walking off the dance floor to other VIP sections with burgundy curtains that closed them off to the rest of the club. Many of them went to a back area of the club to a door that needed a key entry to enter.

"What's in there?"

"Pure bliss," the woman said. "This is a sex club, baby. We come to dance and fuck our brains out. And I would love to fuck you."

The woman leaned forward and grabbed Amira's hand, which she quickly snatched away.

"I—"

"Nautica," a voice said loudly as a small group approached the table. The voice belonged to a man with green hair and gauges in his earlobes. "We've been looking all over this bitch for you. Come on. Some rich white man said if we come with him to the back, he'll get us higher than the sky for a group blow job. Let's go, bitch."

Nautica looked back at Amira and winked. Amira felt the hairs on the back of her neck stand up. There was something about the way Nautica stared at her. Her eyes were filled with a lust Amira had never seen before.

"Maybe next time," Nautica said to her and left the table with her friends.

That fast, Amira lost her appetite. A sex club? As disgusted as she was, she was also intrigued. Tevin ran a sex club. She wondered if he partook in the festivities. The thought made her angry because she suddenly remembered that they hadn't had sex. A man as fine as him had to have been getting it somewhere. No wonder it was easy for him to be patient with her. Her attitude began to consume her, and all she wanted to do was leave. She couldn't stand the thought of looking around at all the beautiful women and wondering if Tevin had dicked them down.

She pushed the menu in front of her away and stood up to see if she could make out Tevin in the crowd of people. However, he wasn't at the bar where the politician had been. In fact, the politician wasn't even there anymore. She sighed and decided to go to the bathroom to check her makeup. She'd taken two steps from the VIP section when a firm hand gripped her arm.

"I thought that was you," a voice she recognized all too well said.

Turning around, she saw Jerron standing there with fire in his eyes. He looked her up and down, seeming to get madder when he saw her outfit. She pulled her arm away from him and mean mugged him as hard as she could. Her face had just healed, and she had finally reached a point where she wasn't looking over her shoulder for him anymore. But there he was when she least expected it. Again.

"Go away, Jerron."

"Not until you tell me what the fuck you're doin' here with that pussy-ass motherfucka Tevin."

"We're together," she said proudly. "He's my man now. And he *doesn't* put his hands on me."

"Yeah, bitch, that's how I know you're crazy. How you got a new dude when I'm still your dude?"

"No, you're not. And Tevin's not going to like the fact that you just grabbed me like that."

"Bitch," Jerron said, wrapping his hand around her neck and pushing her back against a wall. "I'ma kill you before I let another motherfucka have you. Understand?"

"Ooh, kinky, I love it. Get it, girl!" a passerby cheered.

Amira couldn't even speak to signal that she was in real danger. Jerron squeezed tighter and tighter. She tried to claw his face, but it was no use. He was too strong. Her eyesight started to blur, but she still had good enough vision to see Jerron's head snap hard to the side. Suddenly, he let her go, and she gasped for air. Jerron had fallen to the floor, and Tevin stood there with balled fists. He ran up to where Jerron was and continued to punch him until blood was drawn. When he was done, he pulled a pistol from his waist and shoved it in Jerron's mouth.

"Whoa, Tev, chill!" Sparrow ran to where they were fighting. "Too many eyes in here, man. Let it go."

"I'm not letting shit go," Tevin said furiously, staring coldly into Jerron's eyes. "I'm about to kill him."

"Kaleef isn't going to like that, and you know it. Bloodying up his business while he got a case. Let this shit ride for another day, Tev."

Tevin clenched his jaw with his finger on the trigger. Amira didn't know what to do. She gently touched his arm, and it was like her presence brought him back to reality. Slowly, he pulled the gun from Jerron's mouth. But when he did, he got one more lick in. He kicked Jerron so hard in the head that he fell over, knocked out. Afterward, he turned to Sparrow.

"The only reason I didn't take his soul right now is because there are too many witnesses. But know this. This shit is far from over. Come on, Amira. Let's go."

# Chapter 8

Amira was still a little shaken up by what had just happened, but she held it together the best she could when she and Tevin left. It wasn't until they reached his place that she finally let out her frustration. She kicked off her shoes and threw her purse on the couch before she shouted at the top of her lungs.

"Aye, Amira! You good?" Tevin asked, rushing to her and placing his hands on her shoulders.

She stopped shouting and began to breathe hard. She had heard his question, but her anger hadn't subsided enough for her to answer. She wished Tevin had just put a bullet in Jerron's head right then and there. At least then she wouldn't have to worry about him putting his hands on her again. He was a rabid dog that needed to be put down. Amira had never wished death on anyone, and she knew that she would feel the same way when she calmed down.

"I can't believe I ever dealt with him. I don't know what I ever saw in him," she finally said.

However, she *did* know what she saw in him at the time. Jerron was young, exciting, and he could keep up with the lifestyle she was used to, all of which came at a cost that had come due. He wasn't going to let her go, not until he had her by his side. And if he couldn't have her, he had made it very clear that he wasn't afraid to kill her.

"I shoulda handled his ass the first time," Tevin said sadly, cupping her chin. "I'm your man. I'm supposed to protect you."

"You did."

"I didn't. He had his hands around your neck. I shoulda—"

"You got him off me. You saved me, Tevin."

"Fuck that. That poor excuse of a bitch shouldn't have ever even gotten that close to you. He caught me slipping, but it won't happen again."

There was something dark in his tone that gave Amira chills. He meant every word, and she knew things wouldn't be pretty the next time Tevin ran into Jerron. Not wanting him to stay in a bad mood, she wrapped her arms around him and kissed him gently on the lips.

"Did you just call yourself my man?" she asked with a twinkle in her eye.

"Yeah. I'm not?"

"We just haven't made anything official, so I didn't know."

"Well, now you do. I'm falling for you, Amira, and I want you with me . . . if you'll have me."

She smiled big and nodded her head before kissing him again, deeply. The way their tongues danced made her grow hot between her thighs. She wanted him, and that time, just allowing him to give her head wouldn't do. She wanted their bodies to be one.

He seemed to be on the same page as her because before she knew it, he broke the kiss and led her to the back master bedroom. Once there, he scooped her into his arms, and she wrapped her legs around his waist. Their lips reconnected, and his hands ran up her legs and under her skirt. His warm hands felt good as they fondled her bottom, and she grinded her body into his, hoping to turn him on even more. Gently, he laid her down on the bed and looked at her with wonder.

"You're beautiful, Amira. You could have anybody you want. You know that?"

"Yeah, but I want you. And only you. And right now, I want you . . . here."

She spread her legs and moved her thong out of the way so he could see where she was talking about. She rubbed her slippery clit with two fingers while watching his face get more turned on by the second. He wanted her just like she wanted him. It was obvious. But still, he hesitated.

"You sure?" he asked.

"Yes," she said. "First, I want you to make love to me like in the movies. I want to feel how much you really care about me. And then . . . I want you to fuck me like you hate me."

"What?"

"You heard me. Now, come on. There's a flood warning." She grinned and reached up to pull him down on top of her.

When she got home, Amira tried to open and close the front door without making a sound. It was almost midnight, but the lights inside were still on. She didn't know if it was Winnie who was still awake or her father. Either way, she didn't want to answer any questions they may have had. She couldn't wait for the day they didn't treat her like a child that needed to be watched.

She also hadn't told them about Tevin, especially not after how much her dad couldn't stand Jerron. Although he had been right about him, Tevin was different. She didn't want him to be prejudged. When the time was right, she would tell the world about him, but right then, she would enjoy and keep him to herself. She managed to make it up the fifth step when she heard loud shouts from the kitchen area.

"*Shit!*"

The voice belonged to her father, and he sounded angry. She had half a mind to continue up the stairs, but curiosity got the best of her. She fixed her clothes before returning down the stairs and toward the kitchen. When she got to the entrance, she saw that her dad was sitting with his back toward her and on the phone. Winnie was nearby, hurriedly trying to fix him a cocktail. Amira's brow creased. He only drank when he was having a horrible day.

"How wasn't I given a heads-up about this? I pay you good money to let me know what's going on in the bureau. My client is a very dangerous man. You *know* this." He paused to take the cocktail from Winnie and swallowed a big gulp of it. "Yeah, well, next time, try harder. Kaleef Hinton is the biggest name going around over there. You should have known that they were planning to arrest him. Thanks for nothing!"

Aramous disconnected the call and slammed the phone down. Amira made to walk toward him, but Winnie saw her and shook one of her hands no. She then gestured her head as if to tell Amira to leave the kitchen. Amira nodded. She didn't have to be told twice. When her dad was mad, he was like a raging dragon. She took Winnie's advice and rode the high Tevin had given her to her bedroom.

# Chapter 9

Kaleef getting taken down by the Feds caused the motion to be slow in the streets. Things were quiet, and everyone felt they had a target on their backs. Not only that, but also the charges he was facing were steep; so steep, whispers of if he would be getting out began circulating in the different organizations. Many people hadn't paid what they owed, and Sparrow knew it was because the big man was off campus. It was up to him to keep the ball rolling, or so he thought, especially since word on the street was that Eddie Lanes over South was talking big trash about Kaleef.

Eddie had been getting product from Kaleef for years, but it was no secret that the two men didn't care for each other. What they had was a mutually beneficial business relationship. It was no surprise to Sparrow that he was speaking ill of Kaleef while he was down. All it did was leave room for someone to take his place. The streets moved like that, but Sparrow would let everyone know that nothing was changing any time soon.

Sparrow was planning on paying Eddie a visit anyway, but it made the meeting more imperative when he didn't pick up his usual shipment. His order was one of Kaleef's biggest, and he was always on time. It had Sparrow's mind going, and he knew Kaleef wouldn't be happy to hear it. He'd been locked up for a few weeks since the judge denied him bail. Sparrow didn't want to add more bad news on top of what he was already going through. He would handle it himself.

On his way over South, he stopped to pick up Jerron, Zech, and Tay. Zech and Tay were cousins and good for a gunfight. They had come up in Kaleef's organization and had been loyal workers for over a decade. Sparrow trusted them with his life. They got in the back, and Jerron hopped in the passenger seat.

Jerron was a young, hotheaded gritter, but Sparrow had taken a liking to him. He was the type to shoot first and get out of there before questions were asked. He was thorough regarding the drug game and getting money, which was why Sparrow didn't understand how a girl could have his nose wide open like that. Sparrow had seen her with his own eyes. She was bad and all, but there were a million like her. He would never go out sad like Jerron had over some vagina.

"Yo, what the fuck was that at the club the other night?" Sparrow asked as he drove.

He had been busy handling business since Kaleef had been locked up, so he hadn't had time to talk to Jerron about what had happened. Sparrow would have never put his money on Tevin if someone asked who would win in a fight between him and Jerron. However, seeing how easily he dropped him, Sparrow realized he had clearly underestimated the kid.

"What you talking about?" Jerron played dumb.

"You know what I'm talking about. At the club the other night. You and Tevin."

"Huh." Jerron smacked his lips. "Fuck Tevin."

"From how he dropped yo' ass, I would guess it's fuck you too."

"Man, that motherfucka sucker punched me over that bitch!"

Sparrow glanced at him and saw the rage coming over his face. He watched Jerron clench and unclench his jaw muscles. It was clear that Tevin and the girl were a touchy subject for him.

"Who's the bitch anyway?"

"I used to fuck with her, but I cut her loose. She been fucking with Tevin to make me mad."

"You sure that's the story? It looks like she's really feeling him," Sparrow asked doubtfully.

"Yeah. I don't gotta lie about shit. She been on my line begging to come back. But fuck her too."

"A'ight," Sparrow said, dropping the topic.

They had just pulled up to the lounge where they were meeting Eddie. Sparrow nodded in the rearview mirror at Zech and Taylor after they parked. Everyone exited the car and went inside the club.

The pungent aroma of smoke filled Sparrow's nose as they made their way to where Eddie was. He sat in a section in the back surrounded by his own people. Eddie was a dark-skinned man in his early forties who didn't go anywhere not dressed in a suit. He was a clean-cut guy with a clean fade and trimmed beard. He was the type to keep only the sexiest women on his arm, and that day was no different. Two fine specimens sat with him, staring at him like he was a god.

As Sparrow approached, Eddie gestured for them to get up so he could sit down. They did so without a second thought and went to the bar. Eddie's goons, however, stayed put and watched Sparrow like a hawk, which was fine because Jerron, Zech, and Taylor returned the favor.

"Sparrow, how's my favorite number two doing?" Eddie greeted him in his naturally hoarse voice.

"Hmm." Sparrow laughed at Eddie's little dig. "I would be doing better if I knew why you didn't pick up your shipment this month."

"Right to business, I see."

"Right to business."

"You don't want to enjoy your time in this fine club first? All the fine women in here. You could use their company. You look tense," Eddie said, but when he saw the serious look on Sparrow's face was unchanging, he sighed. "Okay, well then, I guess I'll get to the point. Kaleef is in jail."

"Will you answer my question or keep stating the obvious?"

"The obvious is the answer to the question. I don't know if it's wise to continue doing business with someone the Feds have obviously watched. If the tables were turned, do you think Kaleef would keep copping from me?"

"If you think they'll be able to hold him in there, you're a fool. He has the best lawyer in the state. He'll be out soon. And how do you think he'll feel when he learns how quick you were to write him off?"

"Ha. I don't think your boy is getting out of this jam. Like you have eyes and ears on the inside, so do I. And I heard Cheryl Pond is who's testifying against him. And if memory serves me right, she was his old connect, right? He had to have worked a number on her for her to turn on him like this."

"As I said, he won't be in there long," Sparrow repeated, keeping his voice even.

The truth was Kaleef hadn't said anything about Cheryl Pond, leading him to wonder if he even knew. But if what Eddie said was true, then Kaleef's situation was much more serious than he thought. Five years earlier, Cheryl had gotten caught up transporting a big shipment of drugs to the US. It got her a forty-year bid and put Kaleef in the position to deal directly with her family.

"Well, until his situation changes, I will take my business elsewhere. I can't take that kind of risk. You understand, right?"

"Listen, you oversized M&M," Sparrow growled, standing to his feet. Eddie's men gripped at their waists, and so did Sparrow's men. "Kaleef fucked with you when nobody would let you touch their product. And this is how you repay that generosity?"

"Business is business." Eddie shrugged. "But if you want to make it more than that, I'm inclined to tell you that these gentlemen right here aren't the only shooters I have in the building."

Sparrow and Eddie glared at each other. Sparrow was trying to find the bluff, but there was no way to know for sure. Every fiber in his being told him to blow Eddie's roof back, but he had to save that fun for another day. Sparrow motioned for his men to stand down and then turned back to Eddie.

"I'll be seeing you," he said.

"Is that a threat? I *love* those."

Sparrow chuckled and nodded his head before walking away from the table. Men like Eddie were his favorite kind of giant. The sound they made when they fell was satisfyingly deafening. Jerron, Zech, and Taylor followed him back to the car. Sparrow stopped Jerron from getting in but let the others climb in.

"You thinking what I'm thinking?" Jerron asked before Sparrow said a ward.

"Only if you're thinking that Eddie has to go."

"Say no more. It's done."

"Nah, I need this done clean. Not any of that hothead shit you're known for. Nah . . . I need Tevin in on this too."

"I ain't working with that motherfucka," Jerron said, making a face.

"It's not a request," Sparrow said, cutting his eyes at him. "I don't give a fuck if y'all don't like each other. You're going to work together on this. Tevin is the cleanest killer I've ever met. Unlike you, he's calculating, and this is a job I need to be thought out. It has to look like an accident. We don't need a war on our hands. Understand?"

"Yeah, man." Jerron let out a hard breath. "Can't believe you're tryin'a have me work with that clown."

"Hopefully, next time, you think before you start a stupid-ass beef over some pussy."

# Chapter 10

As a man accustomed to his freedom, jail was a bit of an adjustment for Kaleef. It wasn't his first rodeo, but it was his first time being in one so long. He'd had the utmost confidence that Aramous would keep his word and get ahead of the case, but that confidence faded when the Feds arrested him while he was checking the mail. It faded even more with each day he sat in a jail cell.

Cheryl Pond. The name sent anger coursing through his body as a corrections officer led him to his visit. At one point, she had been what some would call his business partner. Through him, she had integrated her family's product through Atlanta and other parts of Georgia. It was a good arrangement . . . until she found herself on the wrong side of the law.

The officer directed Kaleef to a seat with clear glass in front of it. On the other side of the glass was Sparrow. He already had the phone to his ear, so Kaleef picked up his.

"How you holding up in here?"

"It is what it is," Kaleef said, then felt someone hovering over him. Turning his head, he saw that the officer was still standing there. "Aye, do you mind? Give me some fucking space."

"My bad, Kaleef," the officer said and quickly went to stand behind another inmate.

Kaleef shook his head in annoyance, and his friend laughed.

"You're the man wherever you go, I see," Sparrow said.

"I don't want to be the man in here. That's a fool's dream. I'm ready to be a free man. You talk to Aramous?"

"He said he's doing all he can do. The charges against you are pretty steep, and apparently, there's a lot of fucking evidence. What the hell happened, Leef? Who fucked up?"

"Listen, they don't know shit. It's all speculation. And whatever that bitch has to say about me won't be able to stick."

"You mean Cheryl Pond?"

"Her."

"That's what I'm confused about. I thought the Ponds were solid as they came. Why would she suddenly turn snitch?"

"I don't know," Kaleef lied.

He did know, but he didn't understand how Cheryl knew. However, it was the only reason he could think of that she would want him to suffer the same fate as her. Five years earlier, an opportunity came to Kaleef to expand in areas of Georgia that he'd never touched with his product. It was a kingpin's dream. The only thing was, Cheryl didn't trust upping the amount of product her family was already giving him. Nor would she set up a meeting between Kaleef and her father. Even though he always made good on his money, she wouldn't budge.

Kaleef was beginning to feel like an ant under a thumb. That was where Cheryl wanted him to stay. What had started as a fruitful business venture between two bosses soon turned into a dependent situation. Kaleef didn't like that. So, he did what he had to do. He knew he was being investigated for a different charge at that time. At Sunday family dinner, Kaleef let slip that a shipment was being transported to a local warehouse. Days later, a bust happened, and Cheryl, unfortunately, didn't make it out with her freedom. And unfortunately for her father, Sleepy, he didn't make it away from Kaleef with his life.

"Kaleef?" Sparrow said, waving his hand in front of the glass. "You still with me?"

"My bad. I was just thinking. You need to tell Aramous to put some pep in his step and get me the fuck out of here."

"I can tell him all I want, but that won't change the fact that we don't know where Cheryl is. If she's the key to this whole thing, then she gotta go because we need you out here."

There was something about the way he said it that Kaleef didn't like. He raised a brow and studied Sparrow's face.

"What's wrong?"

"It's Eddie."

"What about that suit-wearing motherfucka?"

"He said he doesn't want to cop his product from us anymore. He didn't get his last shipment."

"Why?"

"Shit, in so few words, he said he doesn't want to tie his business to a sinking ship."

As a businessman, Kaleef understood. But as the businessman who had taken a chance on Eddie's broke ass when nobody else would, he was infuriated.

"Is he still alive?"

"For now," Sparrow said simply, and Kaleef nodded, knowing what that meant.

"Listen, when you leave here, I need you to make Aramous work harder. He has connections everywhere. He can find out where Cheryl is."

"And how am I supposed to do that?"

"He just needs a little push, that's all."

"Like an incentive? I can drop some money off to him later."

"Nah, money won't be enough to do this. I need you to take something he loves," Kaleef said, pulling something out of his pocket and pressing it on the glass. "You need to get her."

"Is that—"

"His daughter." Kaleef cut him off, but Sparrow shook his head.

"Nah," he said, looking closer at the photo as if trying to make sense of something. Suddenly, it clicked. "I know her. That's the little bitch Tevin is fucking with. Him and Jerron just got into it over the bitch."

"Tevin, as in my cousin?"

"Yeah. He brought her to the club the other night. They were all hugged up and shit. He's really feeling her. Damn, small world."

"Well, I need you to do what you gotta do. Tevin will understand. Matter of fact, don't even tell him. I don't need anything getting in the way of Aramous's work ethic."

"What you want me to do with her?"

"I don't give a fuck. Put her to work if you have to. I need Aramous to know I'm not playing with his high-sidity ass."

"Say no more."

# Chapter 11

Amira listened to the phone ring and didn't hang up until it went to voicemail. It was the third time she'd called Tevin's phone, and he didn't answer. She was trying not to get an attitude, but it was getting harder and harder. She shot him a text, asking where he was.

"Girl, I have never seen you trip this hard over a boy before," Meka said.

The two of them lay in Meka's bed watching TV. Well, Meka was watching it. Amira was too in her head and wondering why Tevin wasn't answering her calls *or* calling her back. It wasn't like him to do that, and she couldn't stop her mind from wandering. Had he gotten what he wanted from her, and now he was done? She couldn't bear that thought, not with her feelings for him growing so strong.

"It's just not like him to ignore me like this," she whined.

"Maybe he's not ignoring you, crazy. Maybe he's busy."

"Nobody is too busy for me."

"Oh, hell no. You sound like a narcissist."

"Girl, go to hell."

Amira rolled over on her back and looked at the ceiling. Was she being clingy? She knew the kind of business Tevin was in, and there were bound to be times when she wouldn't be able to get in contact with him. It was just that outside of Meka, he was the only person that made her life seem like a life. Things at home were so tense, especially with her father working on his case. She'd never seen him so stressed out behind a client. In her hand, Amira's phone started to ring. When she looked at the caller ID, her heart fluttered when she saw Tevin's name.

"Hello?"

"My bad, baby. I'm in the field," his deep voice came through.

"Mmmm. I thought something happened to you."

"Nah, you know I'm a Titan. It would take Zeus to take me down."

"Here you go," Amira teased with a giggle. Meka sat next to her, rolling her eyes. "When you're done, let's go get some food. I miss you."

"Uhh—"

"*Tevinnnn!*" Amira heard the singsong voice of a woman in his background, and her heart dropped. "*Come here, baby.*"

"Baby? Tevin, who the hell is that?" Amira demanded, and Meka scooted closer to hear what was going on.

"It's nobody," he said.

"Are you fucking with one of those bitches at Tranquility?"

"Amira—"

"Are you?" she asked, and Tevin sighed.

"Chill. I probably won't finish what I'm doing until late, though. Let's link tomorrow."

"You know what? Don't worry about it. Go back to fucking your bitch."

"Amira, wai—"

Amira hung up, and it felt like she was about to throw up. Not Tevin. She never would have thought he would do her like that. But why wouldn't he? They were still in the beginning stages of their relationship. She'd trusted him. Tears welled up in her eyes, but she blinked them away.

"He ain't shit, girl," Meka said, shaking her head.

Amira sniffled, thinking about just lying down and sleeping, but the sadness in her chest soon was replaced with white rage. There was no way she would let another man get away with hurting her. She would find him and give him a piece of her mind. The only place she could think of where he might be was Tranquility. She jumped up from Meka's bed to grab her purse and keys.

"Where are you going?" Meka asked.

"To catch me a cheater," Amira said and was gone.


When she got to Tranquility, she parked and sat there for a moment, staring at the steering wheel. Amira honestly didn't know what she was in for. She hadn't prepared herself for what she would do when she found Tevin. Maybe she just wanted to see with her own two eyes that her knight in shining armor wasn't really a knight at all. He was a dragon, just like Jerron.

Not only that, but also in her fit of rage, she had forgotten that she technically wasn't even old enough to get inside Tranquility. Still, she grabbed her purse and got out, walking to the door. Although it was the middle of the day, the line to get into the club was as long as it was the night she'd been there. She noticed some executive-looking men able to skip the line and go right in after showing security some kind of card.

She walked by the line of people and marched right up to security. They were different from those who were there the night she was with Tevin. Both looked her up and down in her corset top and stacked high-waist pants with smirks on their faces. Amira put a hand on her hip and pointed at the door.

"I need to get in there," she told the guard closest to her.

"No problem, beautiful. You just need to show us your membership card and ID." He held out his hand.

"I don't have those things with me, but I need to get in there."

"I'm sorry, pretty face. No ID, no entrance. Club rules." He shrugged carelessly. "Next."

"I'm the girlfriend of the motherfucka who runs this place. You're going to let me in there."

"I'm going to give you three seconds to—"

"It's cool. I got it," a voice said, coming up behind security. Amira looked and saw it was the same man from that night, Sparrow. "Well, look at what we have here."

"I'm looking for Tevin. Is he here?" Amira asked.

"I don't know. How about we go see? Let her through."

The security did as they were told and let Amira pass them. Sparrow put an arm around her and led her inside the club. It was just as packed as before, but the music wasn't as loud. The crooning from the speakers was soft and sexy. The couples on the dance floor grinded their bodies slowly into each other. There was a nice vibe in the air.

Sparrow took her to the bar. He helped her onto the stool, and she began to look around once she was seated. She didn't see Tevin, but she also knew that there were doors that led to other places inside the club. The image of him in an orgy with multiple women invaded her mind. The voice she'd heard on the phone sounded very sensual. The bartender, a sexy woman wearing a bralette and a short pair of shorts, approached Amira.

"What will you have, doll?"

"Make her our Long Island *Special*. It's on the house," Sparrow told the bartender.

"Coming right up."

She went on to make Amira's drink and left the two of them to talk. Sparrow stared down at Amira with a sparkle in his eyes. She paid him no attention; she just wanted to find Tevin.

"Did you say if Tevin was here?"

"I did not. In fact, I don't think I've seen him today."

"So why would you bring me in here?" Amira made a face at the older man in annoyance.

"Because you looked like you were about to fight my security, and I can't have that. Plus, you seemed like you needed a drink to calm you down. Everything good?"

"I don't know." Amira shrugged. "I heard some girl on the phone when I talked to him and—"

"You came down here to beat up a bitch?" Sparrow asked with a chuckle. "Baby girl, I'll be the first to tell you guys like Tevin aren't the settle-down type. They live a fast life, too fast for just one woman. You might be his main girl, but trust me, there will always be a few on the side. It's just how the game goes."

"You're wrong about him."

"Am I? If I was, you wouldn't be down here . . . right?" Sparrow raised a brow in a knowing way.

To that, Amira had nothing to say. The bartender returned with her drink, and she slurped a huge gulp of it from her straw. Amira had never had a Long Island iced tea, and it was strong. Good, but strong. She took another drink and tried to ignore Sparrow's words. But it was hard to. Maybe he was right.

"By the way you're downing that drink, I can see I struck a nerve," Sparrow said, amused. "Let's talk about other things."

"Like what?"

"Like you."

Amira made another face as she took another drink. Why would he want to know about her? She hoped he wasn't trying to make a pass at her. He was her father's age, and even if he wasn't that old, he wasn't her type. Sparrow was a little too rough around the edges. He dressed nice and smelled good, but everything about him screamed thug.

"What about me?" she asked with a slightly turned lip.

"You're a very special girl, Amira."

The way he said her name made chills run down her spine. She looked into his eyes and saw that they were fixed on her. It gave her a weird feeling in her stomach.

"H-how did you know my name? Tevin didn't tell you. And neither did I."

"I know everyone who comes into my place of business. Especially someone so"—he ran a finger down her cheek—"valuable. Do you know your father is Kaleef's lawyer?"

"What . . . What does that have to do with anything?"

"*Everything,*" he laughed. "Kaleef paid your father a lot of money to ensure what happened didn't happen. Unfortunately, now we must go a different route with things to make Daddy work harder."

Amira didn't like the way the conversation had turned. She felt that it was time for her to leave. If Tevin wasn't there, there was no reason she still was. She got up from the bar stool and began to walk away. On the second step, something felt off. She felt woozy, and her legs were like Jell-O under her. It was like they had forgotten how to function. The next thing she knew, she was swaying back and forth. She was about to lose her footing.

Sparrow grabbed her from behind. "You made this so easy for me. I thought I would have to tear the whole city up to find you. But you came right to me. I guess I'm a lucky man."

Feeling sleepy, Amira said, "What . . . What did you do to me?" as he led her away from the bar.

"Shhh . . . Don't worry about that. I have something special in store for you."

# Chapter 12

"Amira!" Tevin said into the phone, but it was too late. She'd hung up in his face.

He was just about to call her back when a pair of arms wrapped around him, and a set of lips kissed his ear. A flowery perfume snuck up his nostrils, and he heard a giggle. Tevin shrugged the woman off him and turned to face her. With a disgusted expression, he looked down his nose at the half-naked woman.

"I told you the last time I was here. I don't know where the fuck you've been, so don't touch me. Where the fuck is Jerron?"

She was clearly high because all she did was giggle some more. A small stack of money she'd been counting was in one of her hands before she interrupted Tevin's phone call. Her perky breasts jiggled when she shrugged her shoulders as an answer to his question. Tevin didn't put his hands on women, but if he did, she would have been one to get smacked.

"Get the fuck out of my face and get back to work," Tevin told her and pointed for her to go back to the living room with the others.

Tevin was about to search the house but didn't have to. A different girl emerged from the hallway that led to the bedrooms upstairs. She wiped the corners of her mouth and smirked at Tevin as she passed. Shortly after, Jerron came after her.

"Are you ready, or what?" Tevin asked, not impressed at the sight of him.

"Damn, I can't get some head before we go kill a motherfucka?" Jerron scoffed.

If it hadn't come at Kaleef's request, Tevin would have never agreed to do a job with Jerron. At one point, the two had been cordial enough to be around each other sometimes, but there was always something about Jerron that Tevin didn't trust. He was a thoroughbred when it came to business. Tevin would give him that, but Tevin didn't think his humanity was intact, and that was what made him dangerous. But that was fine because Tevin was dangerous too.

"Let's go," he said.

He left the house, and Jerron followed him to his car. The word was Eddie Lanes didn't want to be aligned with Kaleef anymore. The sudden parting of ways would mean a blow to Kaleef's business, which wasn't good for anybody. Tevin had known Eddie since he was a kid. Eddie wasn't a boss back then; he was barely even a worker. Any chance he got, he was begging Kaleef for some work or to put him in position. So when Kaleef did, and he blew like he had, one would think loyalty would be a given. However, some people liked to repay the hand that fed them with a knife to the palm.

Tevin wished Sparrow would have put someone else on the job with him. He kept a level head, though, even though he saw Jerron keep mugging him from the passenger seat. Their personal differences didn't matter at the moment.

"So, where we about to find the foo man?" Jerron asked, finally breaking the silence.

"For the past week, Eddie has been at the same diner every day and at the same time. He either likes the food that much, or something else is happening. I'm thinking about the latter."

"You think that's HQ?"

"Maybe. Every time he goes, he enters through the back. He walks in with a briefcase and walks out with nothing."

"So what am I 'sposed to do with this information? If that's HQ, it gotta be hella motherfuckas guarding that bitch. Sparrow said we have to make it look like an accident. Stupid. I can't believe he sent me on a mission with yo' ass."

Tevin took a deep breath to calm himself.

"Who said anything about killing him there? Shut the fuck up and listen," Tevin said, driving with one hand. "When he leaves without the briefcase, it signifies the end of his day. When he leaves, his security stays at the diner."

"That don't even make sense. Why the fuck would he be naked out here for?"

"I don't know, but I've followed him to a place over South every day for the past week. He gets dropped off at night and picked up in the morning."

"You think it's his bitch's house?"

"Maybe. Whoever's house it is, he's really secretive about it. He doesn't even want his people to know about it. It's about to be five now, so he should be pulling up to the diner. Let's head over South and wait for him."

"If he shows, what's the move?"

"You'll see."

Tevin didn't say another word, and before Jerron could keep talking, he turned the music up. The tension in the car could be cut with a knife. His mind went to Amira. He knew he would have some explaining and making up to do later, which he didn't mind. He enjoyed spoiling her and treating her well. His grandmother had always told him that he had an old soul. He would have to agree. His views on women and dating were different from the men around him.

Tevin didn't want to have a slew of women. He didn't want to have to spread the pieces of himself from person to person. He wanted one woman who he could give his all to. He was young, but he lived fast. There was no telling which day could be his last, so what was the point in living the "young" life when he could just live the life he wanted? Plus, his grandparents had been together since they were fifteen years old. They stayed together for fifty years until his grandpa died, and when he did, Tevin's grandmother never even thought about another man.

"Once you meet the love of your life, your soul knows. And it will never yearn for another." They were his grandmother's words, and ever since he met Amira, he knew they were true. What he felt was deeper than mere attraction with her, and that was why he knew he would do whatever it took to get back in her good graces.

He and Jerron drove to the house he'd followed Eddie to, and they parked across the street.

"What now?" Jerron asked.

"Look," Tevin said and pointed at the house.

A tall woman stepped out of the house and locked the door behind her. Tevin got a good look at her even from where they were parked. It wasn't a woman at all. It was a man dressed as a woman.

"What the fuck?" Jerron said incredulously beside Tevin. "This motherfucka is gay?"

"It's looking like it."

"It looks like he/she is about to leave. We just supposed to wait here?"

"Yup. My grandma used to tell me that one thing a man can't shake is a habit and a fetish. He'll be here."


Aramous paced back and forth in the kitchen while rubbing his hand down on his face. He was waiting on one of his connects to give him a callback with details about the Kaleef Hinton case. He had never been so stressed out about a job. He feared he would have to move or get security to surround his house if he didn't get something sorted out soon. Kaleef was a very powerful man, and Aramous had to admit he'd acted in a cocky manner with the case. He thought they were smooth sailing, and being blindsided with Cheryl Pond was the last thing he expected.

He had no idea where she was since they pulled her from the prison where she was doing her bid. They must have known how much influence Kaleef had. She was a sitting duck in a prison cell. It was like she'd fallen off the face of the earth because he couldn't get a lock on her no matter who he reached out to. He paused from pacing to pour himself a shot of Jack on the rocks. When he took a swig, the burning in his chest was almost therapeutic. However, when his phone rang, he was brought right back to reality. He scrambled to answer it, thinking it was his guy at the bureau.

"Dave, did you get the info I need?" Aramous answered the phone without looking at the caller ID.

"This ain't Dave, Aramous." A deep voice came through the phone.

"Who is this?"

"A messenger. Kaleef needs you to work harder."

"Kaleef hired me, but he's not my boss. I'm working as diligently as I can to get him out of jail."

"Well, he feels that you aren't working hard enough. He feels you need more motivation."

"What's that supposed to mean?" He heard a commotion in the background, like a struggle was ensuing. "Hello?"

"Daddy? Daddy, is that you?"

It was Amira. Hearing his daughter's voice sound so feeble made his entire body turn as cold as ice. The hand holding the glass of Jack shook so furiously that he could hear the ice hitting the glass.

"A-Amira?"

"Daddy, please come get me. Please. They—"

"That's enough." The man who had called Aramous got back on the phone. "Now, do you see how serious Kaleef is? And if you go to the law, she's dead. Don't forget we have moles. You have twenty-four hours to find Cheryl Pond and seventy-two hours to get his charges dropped. Understand?"

"Yes, yes. I understand. Just please don't hurt my daughter."

"That all depends on you. The clock starts now."

The phone went dead.

"*Fuck!*" Aramous shouted and threw his glass at the wall.

"What? What happened?" Winnie shouted, running into the kitchen.

"Winnie, they have Amira. They have my baby!" Aramous said in a desolate tone and dropped to his knees.

"Oh no. No, no . . ."


Closing the front door of the house, Eddie grinned and rubbed his hands together. He was ready to get a helping of his favorite dessert. Cupcake was her name, and pleasing him was the game. She was still out and about, but when she got back, he had a treat for her, which came in the form of hundred-dollar bills.

Cupcake wasn't a regular woman; she was transgender. And that meant she could please him in ways others couldn't. She also respected his need for discretion. She knew who he was in the streets and how important being low-key was. Plus, she wasn't about to do anything to jeopardize her Benjamins.

Walking through the house, he juggled the burger and fries he brought home for Cupcake from the diner, a bottle of Champagne, and a shopping bag. The bag contained the getup he wanted her to wear for the night ahead. He placed the Champagne and the food on the kitchen counter and went up the stairs toward the bedroom. Not knowing how much time he had, he wanted to shower and clean up for her.

He stripped out of his clothes when he entered the master bathroom and turned on the shower. Stepping in, he relished the feeling of the hot water on his skin. He was just getting into his groove when he heard a noise from the bedroom. At first, he ignored it, but then it happened again. Eddie stuck his head out of the shower curtain to hear more clearly. Someone was definitely in the house with him. He smiled.

"Baby, you see the Champagne and food downstairs?" he called out. There was no answer. "Baby?"

Again there was no answer. He didn't think anything of it. In fact, he smiled harder. Cupcake loved to role-play, and he was excited to see what she had in store. He finished in the shower and got out, wrapping a towel around his waist. He didn't bother to dry off and tracked water on her wooden floors.

"Cupcake?" he said when he stepped out of the bathroom and into the bedroom. She wasn't there. "Baby, stop playing. I want to see you. I missed you."

He left the room and went into the dimly lit hallway. He was by the stairs when the door to the hallway closet swung open. A masked assailant hopped out with a gun pointed at him.

"Sorry, I'm not Cupcake, you nasty motherfucka."

"What the fuck?" Eddie shouted, surprised.

Another masked man ran up, appeared from behind him, and put a gun to the back of his head. He was so taken aback that he didn't know what to do. There he was, caught up with a towel on between two intruders. His gun was in the bedroom. He didn't know what else to do but put his hands up.

"I-I have money—about five thousand. You can have it all," he told them. Cupcake would just have to be mad at not getting her payment.

"Bitch, we aren't here for your money. We're here as a courtesy to Kaleef."

"Kaleef?"

"Yeah, Kaleef. But if he knew you were into this sick-ass shit, I'm sure he would have sent us here to kill you sooner. I'm so disgusted I should just—"

"Chill," the other masked assailant said as the man in front of Eddie raised his gun to pistol-whip him. "Not like that."

"Then how?" the angry one asked.

"Wait, wait. Tell Kaleef I was only playing with him," Eddie begged. "I'll be getting my order tomorrow. I would never forget all he did for me."

"It's too late for that," the calmer out of the two told him. "Goodbye, Eddie."

Eddie tried to swing on at least one of them, but his attempt was futile. He was shoved, and as he fell back, he lost his footing. He toppled down the stairs like a rag doll. His neck broke on the way down, and he was dead by the time he hit the first level.

Tevin and Jerron ran out of Cupcake's house to the car and pulled off. When they were far enough away, they snatched off the masks from their faces. Before they left, Tevin made sure Eddie was dead. Kaleef would be happy to know that he was out of the picture. Jerron had almost messed everything up by pistol-whipping Eddie, though. If he had had any other signs of bruising, his death could have been ruled a homicide instead of an "accidental" death.

Jerron leaned back in his seat as Tevin drove and looked over at him. "Now that that's out of the way, on to other matters," Jerron said. "Amira. You need to step off."

"Says who? The motherfucka I dropped the other night?"

"That was a lucky shot, and you know it. But as far as Amira goes, your time is up, understand?"

"Nah, it's not *my* time that's up. It's *yours*."

The bullet from Tevin's gun caught Jerron in the temple, causing him to slump instantly. He'd done his duty by doing the job with Jerron like Kaleef wanted, but it was over, and Tevin wasn't about to let his presence keep stinking up his car. Not only that, but he refused to let Jerron speak Amira's name again, not when he had hurt her the way he had. He pulled over to a remote location and dumped Jerron's body before casually driving home to call Amira.

# Chapter 13

"Wake up."

Amira felt a cold splash of water hit her face. She stirred and tried to come to, but her eyes wouldn't open. Her body felt so tired and weak that it took all her energy just to *try* to wake up. Another wave of water was just what she needed to open her eyes. She coughed and choked on the water. Her vision was blurry at first, but when she could focus, she realized she was in a room that wasn't hers. The last thing she remembered was being drugged and talking to her father on the phone.

When her vision cleared, she could make out some of her surroundings. She was in a canopy bed similar to her own, but she knew it wasn't. The room was smaller, and the only decorations on the wall were framed bondage images. In fact, many sex toys were scattered all around the room. Whips, chains, cuffs . . . everything. Standing over her was Sparrow holding a small empty bucket. He grinned down at her in triumph.

"W-where am I?" she asked slowly, sitting up in the wet bed.

"My playhouse," he told her.

"Let me go," she said, trying to stand. Whatever he'd drugged her with hadn't seemed to wear off yet. Her legs still did not work. As soon as she stood up, she fell right back onto the bed. He laughed at her and shook his head.

"You won't be going anywhere until your dad does what Kaleef needs him to do. Until then, I have some fun planned for you."

His voice was loud in her ears, so she heard every word. Slowly but surely, she understood that she was his slave. She found herself wondering if Tevin knew about what was happening to her. Had he just gotten close to her to set her up?

"W-where's Tevin? I want to talk to . . . to talk to Tevin."

"Tevin is busy at the moment," Sparrow told her.

"Does he know I'm here? He'll kill you."

"Tevin ain't gonna do shit to me. He'll mourn you like the rest if your dad doesn't do what he's told."

So he didn't know. It gave her a tiny piece of comfort to know he wasn't a part of such an evil scheme. But as quickly as the comfort came, it left, only to be replaced by terror and dread. Sparrow grabbed her chin, but Amira smacked his hand away. It made him mad. Mad enough to backhand her with a force that sent her flying to the side. A metallic taste hit her tongue, and she realized he'd busted her lip. It was blood. She held her mouth, and when he made like he was going to hit her again, she flinched hard.

"No!"

"Then get with the program. You aren't going anywhere, and outside this door are two men with really big guns. So, get comfortable."

"W-what am I supposed to do? W-what will happen to me if my dad doesn't do what you need him to do?"

As soon as the question left her mouth, Amira regretted it. A sick smile spread across Sparrow's lips. He reached a hand out toward her corset top and undid the top hook. She tried to push his hand away, but he balled it into a fist, and she cringed. Knowing he was bigger and stronger than her, she clenched her eyes shut while he undid each hook. When he was done, she felt cold air brushing against her bare nipples. He cupped one of her breasts with his hand and fondled her.

"Mmm, damn. I see why those young motherfuckas were fighting over you. You're fine as shit."

"Just . . . Just get it over with. Hurry up," Amira said with tears running down her face.

"That's where you have me wrong. I don't have to force any woman to fuck me. I get more turned on when she's enjoying herself. And you? You're going to enjoy this." Sparrow laughed and stepped away from her. "Send her in!"

Amira opened her eyes when she heard the room door open. The person who walked in was the last person she expected to see. It was the girl named Nautica from the other night. In her hands, she had another Long Island.

"Laya at the bar said you wanted me to bring this up here," she said and handed it to him.

"Thank you," he said, holding it up to Amira's mouth. "Drink. It will loosen you up for the fun we're about to have."

She looked from Nautica to Sparrow. She knew what was in the drink but didn't feel like she had a choice. Plus, she wanted to be numb for whatever was about to come next. She wrapped her lips around the straw and gulped the drink, much to Sparrow's satisfaction.

"Damn, Amira, slow down. You're going to pass out before the fun starts," Sparrow said, taking the drink away from her.

He backed away again and sat in a chair in the corner of the bedroom. Nautica looked at him, and he waved his hand, allowing her to approach Amira. Amira felt the effects of the drugs kicking in. She saw Nautica coming to her, but the movements seemed so fluid. Nautica smiled and licked her lips as she stared at Amira's bare breasts. She pushed Amira gently back so she would lie down on the still-damp bed. Amira felt Nautica kissing her face, neck, and nipples. Each kiss sent an electrical jolt through her body. It felt magical but wrong. When Nautica pulled Amira's pants and thong off, Amira began to whisper.

"Tevin. Tevin, please save me."

Nautica heard her and stopped. She made a face and turned her head toward Sparrow behind her. He'd gotten comfortable in the chair and had unzipped his pants. His thick third leg was in his hand, and he stroked it as he watched the girl-on-girl action in front of him.

"Are-are you sure she's okay with this?" Nautica asked. "You told me this is what she wanted."

"It's what she wants because *I* said it's what she wants. Now continue before you're in the same position as her."

Nautica hesitated and looked back down at Amira. She was still conscious, and she'd begun to rub her hands all over herself. The drink had officially kicked in. Nautica had had the concoction, which always made her hornier than ever. The two women locked eyes, and Nautica could see the drug lust in Amira's. She did as she was told and undressed until she too was fully naked. She then leaned down to kiss Amira on the lips. Amira kissed her back and opened her legs, allowing Nautica entry. Nautica kissed her down to her love button and wrapped her lips around it. It tasted sweet, just like she thought it would. Gripping Amira's thighs, she buried her head deeply between them, and soon, the room was filled with nothing but the moans of Amira and Sparrow.

# Chapter 14

It had been almost two days since Tevin had seen or heard from Amira. He knew she was angry with him, but he couldn't see her being so angry that she wouldn't pick up the phone, not even once. He'd run out of options and couldn't take the silent treatment anymore, so he pulled up to her house.

She'd told him where she lived a few times, but it was his first visit there. She told him her father was a judgmental hard-ass, so she didn't want the two to meet. He understood. He would be just as protective if he had a daughter as beautiful as Amira. He pressed the button again when nobody came to the door off the first doorbell ring. Moments later, the door flew open. An older Black lady stood in the doorway, looking like she hadn't slept in days.

"Can I help you?" she asked in an exhausted tone.

"You must be Winnie. Amira told me a lot about you. Is she here?" His question seemed to strike a nerve. Before he knew it, she had tears in her eyes and clutched her stomach. "Ma'am, are you okay? I'm sorry. I can come back later. I just wanted to talk to Amira. I haven't heard from her in a few days."

She began to sob, and Tevin was more confused than ever. He didn't know what he had said that was so wrong. Suddenly, a tall gentleman joined her in the foyer. He took her hands and gave her a concerned look.

"Is everything okay, Winnie?" he asked.

"He . . . He was asking about Amira. I'm sorry, Aramous, sir. I just broke down."

"About Amira?" Aramous turned to Tevin quickly and snatched him up by the shirt. "How the hell do you know my daughter? Are you the one who took her?"

"I'm her . . . Wait, what do you mean 'took her'?" Tevin said, pulling forcefully away from Aramous's grasp. "What the fuck do you mean 'took her'? Talk. I'm Tevin, her boyfriend."

Aramous looked at his own hands before shakily bringing them to the top of his head.

"They . . . They took my baby. They took her. It's my fault."

"Aramous, don't speak like that. It's not your fault."

"Yes, it is, Winnie. Kaleef took her because he felt it was my fault that he was in jail. And I can't find where the fuck the bitch testifying against him is being held. If I don't find her, he will kill Amira tomorrow."

"Wait, what are you talking about? How do you know Kaleef?" Tevin asked.

Aramous paused to look Tevin up and down. The anger spread on his face had turned to desperation and defeat. His shoulders slumped, and he pinched the part of his nose in between his eyes.

"I'm his lawyer."

Tevin let his words sink in. He was getting too much information at once and trying to keep up. Amira was the love of his life. Her father was Kaleef's lawyer. Kaleef was in jail, and he blamed Amira's father. Amira was kidnapped. Kaleef had the love of Tevin's life kidnapped. She was kidnapped. It echoed over and over in his head.

"Fuck," was all he could say when things came full circle. "Fuck."

"Baby, it's a lot. Come in," Winnie said and tried to motion Tevin to enter the house.

"Nah. I gotta go."

"You're upset. You don't need to drive like that. Come in."

"No, you don't understand. I know Kaleef."

"You work for him, don't you?" Aramous asked.

"He's my cousin," Tevin admitted, and Aramous made like he was going to grab him again, but Tevin evaded him. "It's not what you think. I had nothing to do with this."

"Yeah, right! Fuck this. I'm calling the police."

"No. I know Kaleef, and I think you do too. He's a killer. If you do that, Amira is as good as dead. Let me fix this. I'ma find her and bring her home, I promise."

He turned away from the entrance and ran to his car. He had planned on telling her that she would never have to worry about Jerron again. He had handled it. But it looked like he was the one who would be worried. He drove away from Amira's house, not knowing where to look first. There were so many places around the city where Kaleef could have her holed up. He would check them all if he had to. He had to get her back. He couldn't get the defeated look of Aramous out of his mind. He knew it would be a look he mirrored if he didn't find her.

The first place he stopped was one of Kaleef's traps. It was low-key and didn't have much traffic coming in and out. It was used as more of a stash house for anything Kaleef needed hidden for a short time. Tevin ran to the bench on the front porch and felt underneath the seat for the key. When he found it, he hurried to open the door and burst through it.

"Amira?" he shouted, running through it like a mad-man. "Amira!"

He checked every room and closet. All he found were bags of guns and money. She wasn't there. He didn't have time to feel defeated. He left the house and drove to the next one on his mental list. When she wasn't there, he went to the next one. The thought of her tied up somewhere was making his heart break by the second. If Kaleef knew she was his girl, she would have been off-limits. He couldn't help but place some blame on himself. As he drove to another spot Amira could have been stashed at, his phone rang in his pocket. He let it ring to voicemail. However, seconds after it stopped ringing, it started up again.

"Hello?" he answered in an annoyed tone.

"Tevin?"

"Who is this?" he asked, not recognizing the woman's voice.

"Nautica, from Tranquility," she said in a whisper. "I . . . I met you the other night. You were with a girl."

"How did you get this number?"

"I got it from one of the security guards there. I . . . I have something to tell you about your girl. Amira."

Tevin slammed on the brakes and pulled over in traffic. He removed the phone from his ear to look at it, trying to make sure he had heard right. After getting himself together, he returned the phone to his ear.

"What about Amira? You know where she is?"

"Y . . . yes. She's here at Tranquility. She came here looking for you the other day and . . ."

"And what? Spit it out."

"Sparrow took her. He won't let her leave. He's keeping her drugged up, and I don't know why. He made me . . . um . . . and when I did, she said, 'Tevin, please save me.' I think . . . I think he's going to kill her. You need to get up here."

Tevin disconnected the phone and dropped it in the passenger seat. White fury raced threw him as he hit a U-turn in traffic and hit the gas in the direction of Tranquility. A sick feeling filled his stomach, knowing that Sparrow had her at Tranquility. Tevin knew what kind of men came through there, and Amira was just the kind of girl they were looking for. If Sparrow had harmed a hair on her head or allowed anyone else to, his body would be in the same ditch he left Jerron in.

# Chapter 15

Sparrow tried Jerron's line for the third time, but again, it rang through to voicemail. He was getting more and more frustrated. Usually, Jerron called him immediately after a job, but Sparrow was still out of the loop regarding Eddie. He tried Tevin's phone too but got no answer. He wondered if something had gone wrong, but nobody was saying anything. He was in the dark.

"I knew I should have just handled that shit myself." Sparrow shook his head.

He was standing at the bar in Tranquility, waiting for Laya to finish making the drink he requested. He had a lot of pent-up frustration that needed to be released, and he knew just the way to do it. Every man in the world had a kink, and Sparrow's was watching women have sex with each other. Nobody could please a woman like another woman. They naturally knew how to make each other reach a fast climax just by touching the right spot. Watching such artistry made him weak and horny. All he wanted to do was sit in the corner and stroke his own orgasm out. He was excited to watch Amira in action again. Her body was immaculate, and he couldn't lie. This time he planned to join in on the fun.

Laya handed him the drink, and he dropped a crisp hundred-dollar bill on the bar. She snatched it up quickly and winked at him before serving her other customers. He left the main floor of the club and entered the members-only part of the club. The moment he arrived, it was

like a new world opened up. The red lights had an alluring effect, and he saw pure bliss everywhere he turned.
He passed an open curtain, revealing an older white gentleman getting his dick sucked by a naked woman while
another snorted a bump of coke out of his belly button.
Sparrow chuckled when he recognized that it was the
governor. There was no doubt in his mind that Kaleef
would be out of jail soon. He had the entire city eating out
of the palm of his hand. Sparrow took a quick photo with
his phone and went about his business.

He turned a few corners until he reached the Play
Room. It was where he was keeping Amira hidden away.
There was an "under construction" sign outside the room
because they planned to renovate it and add a full bathroom. Sparrow nodded at the two men standing outside
of the door. They moved out of the way and let him pass.
He opened the door and saw Amira lying where he had
left her, and she wasn't alone. One of Sparrow's favorite
treats, Treasure, was in bed with her. She wasn't wearing
anything but a G-string and high heels.

Nautica had refused to come back for round two.
Sparrow felt she knew something was off, and he planned
to deal with her. He didn't need any whistle-blowers
around him. But he would do that later. He wanted to
have some fun first. Treasure was an Ethiopian goddess.
Her long hair flowed around her heart-shaped face, and
her big, cherry-red lips protruded, asking him to kiss
them. She had a petite frame but was thick in all the
places that mattered.

"It took you long enough." She smiled sexily. "This girl
isn't much fun. She's just lying here."

"Oh, trust me. She's about to get lit in a second,"
Sparrow said, holding up the drink.

He went over to Amira and forced her to sit up. He'd
given her a pink lace lingerie set to wear, and seeing it

excited him. She looked at the drink and seemed to know what time it was. She grabbed it from him and began to gulp it down. It hadn't taken much to break her, but he didn't think it would. A spoiled princess like her had never had to withstand anything or get her hands dirty. She would do anything to stay alive and not be hurt.

While she was drinking, Treasure crawled to where he stood and unzipped his pants. He placed his gun to the side so she could have full access. She gave an excited squeal when she pulled his dick out and instantly wrapped her lips around it. Sparrow gripped the back of her head and guided her mouth down his shaft until he felt his tip hit the back of her throat. He moaned when he heard her gagging on it and then proceeded to fuck her face. She sucked and slurped on him real wet and sloppy, just how he liked it.

"Mmm, fuck," he moaned and massaged his own balls. He removed himself from her mouth and pointed at Amira. "Eat her pussy."

Treasure wiped her mouth and giggled. Amira lay on her back without prompting so Treasure could position her head between her legs. Sparrow's dick was still soaked from Treasure's mouth. He stood there jacking off, watching Treasure's tongue flick Amira's clit. At first, the licks were slow, but then they sped up.

"Shit, that pussy is getting wetter and wetter. You like that shit, girl. Don't act like you don't. Mm, mm, mmm."

What he said was true. Amira's body naturally reacted to being pleased by Treasure. Soon, Treasure's chin was soaked, and Amira's body squirmed under her. Sparrow jerked the tip of his one-eyed monster and sighed when Amira's first moan left her lips. He couldn't take it anymore. He had to dive in.

"Move," he said and pushed Treasure out of the way. "Lie right here and play with yourself."

Treasure did as she was told and lay next to Amira. She massaged her own clit while Sparrow positioned himself between Amira's legs. He rubbed her slippery slit with his thumb and trembled at how good he knew it would feel inside her.

"You're going to love this," he said and prepared to slide into her.

Suddenly, he heard a commotion outside of the door. There were shouts and many thuds, followed by two gunshots. Treasure screamed. She and Amira scooted to the top of the bed, holding their knees. Sparrow pulled his pants back up and grabbed his gun. Creeping to the door, he aimed his weapon, prepared for whatever was about to happen. However, as soon as he got close enough, someone kicked in the door with a force that knocked him back. His gun flew from his hand and went flying across the room. Standing there looking like a madman out for vengeance was Tevin. He was pointing his gun directly at Sparrow's dome.

"Tevin, what the fuck are you doing?" Sparrow asked, surprised.

"Wondering what the fuck you got going on," Tevin said and looked at Amira. "Why the fuck is my girl back here, man?"

"Kaleef ordered it. Now put the gun down, cuz. You don't even have to do all that." Sparrow tried to reason with him.

"Fuck that. What kind of sick shit you got going on here?"

"Kaleef told me to get her, so I got her."

"He didn't tell you to rape her, though!" The more he talked, the angrier Tevin became.

"I didn't rape her. I swear I didn't. Put the gun down, cuz."

"I'm not your cuz. The fuck outta my way," Tevin said and passed Sparrow to get to Amira.

"Aye, what the hell do you think you're doing?"

"Taking my girl home. And I'ma deal with you later."

"You can't. Kaleef—"

"If Kaleef knew she was my girl, he would have never told you to do no shit like this," Tevin said, lowering his weapon to attempt to scoop up Amira.

"The funny thing is, he did know. I told him. And he still told me to snatch her up and do whatever I wanted to her."

Sparrow took advantage of the lowered gun and sent a blow to the back of Tevin's head. Tevin was forced to let go of Amira, who fell to the floor. He aimed his gun at Sparrow and fired it, but he missed. Sparrow knocked the weapon away and punched Tevin in his face, making him drop the gun. Then he tried to grab it, but Tevin regained his footing and tackled him. A fight between them ensued on the floor, and Tevin got his licks back, plus more. Sparrow had power, but Tevin had both strength and youth on his side. He easily got the better of the older man and soon had him where he wanted him. Sparrow felt the anguish in the blows Tevin sent crashing into his face. Suddenly, a crack sounded, and Sparrow knew his nose was broken, and he felt the rush of warm blood spilling over his face. When Tevin knew Sparrow was immobile, he stopped hitting him and stood at his feet. Slowly, he grabbed his gun from the floor. Sparrow watched him with the one eye that wasn't swollen shut. First, Tevin aimed the weapon at Treasure.

"I'm sorry. You just look like a talker," he said breathlessly.

"Wait, n—"

The shot from his gun silenced her forever. Tevin then returned to Sparrow. He knelt and placed the barrel of his weapon under his chin.

"Your services are no longer needed."

With one final shot, Sparrow's light was put out forever.

# Chapter 16

*Three months later . . .*

"Baby, you forgot something."

Tevin was on his way out the door when he heard Amira call his name. He looked back to see her rushing to him from the kitchen in their new house. She was beautiful, although her face was bare, her hair was messy, and she wore nothing but a robe. He wondered if she knew how blessed he felt to come home to her every day.

"What I leave?" he asked, checking his pockets for his phone and car keys.

"Me!" she said with a grin and kissed his lips.

When she pulled away and he looked down into her eyes, he couldn't help but give her another one. She was the strongest woman he knew besides his grandmother. The horror she had lived was brief, but still, it was traumatic. However, somehow, she stood there with a smile.

"You good?" he asked her. "'Cause I don't have to go."

"I'm good, Tevin," she reassured him. "You can't stay here with me forever. Plus, you have Jay outside. He won't let anything happen to me while you're gone. I'll be okay."

"All right. You talk to your dad?"

"Yeah, he's still a little mad that I moved out, but he's coming around. After what happened, he's still a little shaken up."

After Tevin had gotten Amira back, he thought it was best that she stay with him. It wasn't something that was up for debate. Both Aramous and Tevin played a dangerous game, but Tevin knew he had better resources to protect Amira. However, that didn't mean Aramous didn't have an important part to play. He dropped Kaleef as a client and never looked back. With Kaleef in jail and Sparrow dead, Tevin was now in charge, and both Amira and her father were off-limits.

Amira didn't want to talk much about what happened to her. She told Tevin what she could remember, and he dropped it after that. He, however, was happy that she was seeing a therapist every week to help her sort out anything she needed to sort out. The biggest thing for him was that he didn't want her to feel that what Sparrow did to her made him look at her any differently. In fact, it made him tighten up in every way. He stopped doing business with the Ponds entirely and found a new connect in Florida. It wasn't hard to get people to fall in line. He was the new made man, and keeping the money flowing was the main focus.

"I'll be back in a bit," he told her. "Be dressed when I get back so we can go eat and shop."

"Shopping? Ooh, baby, yes. I saw that new Chanel purse that I want," she squealed and hugged him tight. She pulled away from him and gave him a serious look. "Tevin, don't forget to *not* take your gun inside that place, okay? I need you to come home."

"I'll never lack like that." He grinned and kissed her once more before stepping out of the house.

He walked to his new Chevy Tahoe and got in. He was the new kingpin, but he still had his old ways. He didn't need to be too flashy. He always wanted to blend in and be out of the way. As he drove by, he waved to Jay, who sat parked on the street outside the house. Tevin knew Amira was in safe hands.

The ride to the jail was long, but it gave him the time he needed to get his thoughts together. He hadn't seen or spoken to Kaleef the entire time he was locked up. Kaleef called, but Tevin changed his number. He didn't have anything to say to his cousin. Many would look at Tevin as choosing a woman over his blood, but in his eyes, Kaleef crossed him first. Tevin would never harm something Kaleef loved, no matter the situation he was in. Tevin had been loyal to Kaleef and done the unimaginable for his cousin, so for Kaleef to do something like that to Tevin when his back was against the wall showed him that he would do anything. Everybody was dispensable.

When he got to the jail, he put his gun in the glove compartment and went inside. The officers inside patted him down and used the metal detector on him before leading him to the visitor station. Kaleef was already there waiting for him. His cousin smirked when he saw Tevin approach and sit down.

Kaleef had been in jail for three months but still looked clean-cut as ever, even in his jail uniform. He also didn't look like he was missing any meals. He picked up the phone, and Tevin did the same.

"Long time no talk, cuz. I was beginning to think you forgot all about me. How you been?"

Tevin stared at him. Kaleef's voice was chipper like he hadn't done what he'd done.

"I've been good," he finally answered.

"Good. I heard about what happened to Sparrow. Whoever did that will have to answer to me when I get out of here." He gave Tevin a knowing look.

Tevin understood Kaleef knew it was him who killed Sparrow. He hadn't made it a secret. He wanted everyone to know what would happen if they ever tried him like that again. It was his turn to smirk.

"You might want to watch your words. I heard dude is a monster," he responded.

Kaleef laughed and leaned closer to the glass that separated them.

"You think you're big shit, huh?" he scoffed. "You crossed me behind a bitch? We're blood."

"She's not just a bitch. I love her. And you knew she was my girl. So who crossed who?" Tevin asked.

"When I get out of here—"

"You're gonna kill me? Make me pay? You must not know."

"Know what?"

"*I'm* running shit now," Tevin said and watched Kaleef's face drop. "Out with the old and in with the new. I heard your lawyer dropped you and picked up a more . . . fruitful client. One who knows how to treat him."

"You motherfucka," Kaleef exclaimed when Tevin winked at him, letting him know exactly who that client was. "You don't know how much you've fucked up for me, Tevin. I'ma make you pay for this. Soon as I'm out of here, I'm on your ass."

"I'm counting on it. When and *if* you get out, you'll have to see me for what you did. Until then, I got the streets on lock. And you? Don't drop the soap. I heard they have a thing for light-skinned, pretty boys."

He hung up the phone as Kaleef continued to shout curses at him. He was hysterical, and when he started to beat on the glass, the officers had to come and detain him. Tevin's last sight of Kaleef was them dragging him away, and he smiled. With Kaleef's power and influence, Tevin was sure there would come a day when he was free. And when that time came, Tevin would be ready.

# Murder

by

*Katt*

# Chapter 1

*I knew at the beginning of this quest exactly how it would end, but still, I welcomed it. My path had a purpose . . . vengeance.*

My mother's name was known widely around the city of Chicago. Chleo Love is what they called her because no matter how much money she had or how much pull she held in the streets, she always showed love. She was bred from them and knew what it was like to be on the other side of the fence. She had run away from home at the ripe old age of 16, trying to escape her mother's abusive ways and the eyes of the men her mother had in and out of their house. Although young, she'd developed a grown woman's body, so with the streets as her new mother, she began turning tricks to survive. She had long, curly brown hair, hazel, doe-shaped eyes, full lips, and high cheekbones that made her look like a model. Even though she was green to the game, my mother wasn't stupid. She knew all about the common street whore and refused to be anything like that. She went into business by herself, with no pimp. She left an abusive household and vowed that no one would ever put their hands on her for control again. Once she realized the value of her unique looks, being of African American and Caucasian descent, she began making a good enough profit to make a living.

When she was 19, she fell in love with one of her tricks. Jared "Smooth" Thompson was a 24-year-old African

American and Irish man with red hair, who promised to show her a life filled with real love outside of prostitution but still with never-ending money. As it turned out, Smooth had a hand dipped deeply in the drug trade business in Chicago, and soon, my mother found out precisely what it was like to play wifey and live out a hood fairy-tale life. Smooth took care of my mother and loved her despite her past. He taught her everything there was to know about the business, and the two spent many happy years together.

The day my mother found out she was pregnant was the same day the love of her life was taken from her forever. Nobody knew what happened at that business-meeting-gone-wrong, but not even five bullets lodged into Smooth's upper body could stop him from coming home like he always promised every day. My mother told me he stumbled into their front yard, and she held his head in her lap in the grass while he lay dying. He held on long enough to tell my mother all of his stash spots and the information to his connect. He heard my mother tell him they were expecting a child, and he made her promise to keep it a secret with his last breath. She always told me that he died with a smile on his face.

When Smooth died, my mother barely had time to mourn. She had to hurry and put in work before a thirsty hustler tried to snatch Smooth's spot on the come-up. It came to be known that Smooth hadn't even told his right-hand man the information he told my mother, which meant his empire was rightfully hers. The ones loyal to Smooth stayed faithful to my mother, and although the city had lost a king, the business had to continue as usual.

My mother kept her promise and kept me a secret. The only person who knew about me was the housekeeper, Neffy, who was around my mother's age. My mother even purchased a second home for me to live in with

Neffy. She told me the resemblance between Smooth and me was too uncanny. One look at my red hair and the connection would be made.

Growing up, I never understood why I had to be kept a secret. I never understood why I couldn't play with the other kids or why my school was almost an hour away. But as I grew, my mother put me up on game. I was always a smart kid. I knew my mother didn't work an ordinary job, and we were rich. I was driven around in a limo whenever I left home to go somewhere, and I had the best of everything.

The day I opened her bedroom door without knocking and saw her loading a pistol and saw a whole brick of cocaine on the table in front of her was the day she broke everything down to me. I was 16. She told me that I had to be kept a secret because nobody knew what happened the night my father was killed, and she promised him that no one would ever know about his only child. She also told me how we got all our money and that one day, the entire empire my father had built would be mine. She then gave me the pistol, instructed me to go on the balcony outside her room, and empty the clip in the sky. Intrigued, I grabbed the gun and did as I was told. When the deed was done, I looked back at her with a grin, only to be surprised by the grim look in her hazel eyes.

"What goes up must come down, Fire." She called me by my nickname and averted her eyes to the sky. "You just took your first life."

Her words mortified me, but I understood the meaning behind them. I dropped the smoking gun and stared at my mother, knowing she had just initiated me without my knowledge. The next day on the news, a woman was reported dead in the street beside her car. The newscaster said the angle that the bullet was lodged in her head proved that it had come from the sky. My mother had been right . . . I'd just taken my first life. When guilt began to plague my 16-year-old mind, my mother ended it quickly. She told me innocent people died every day and that there would be many more bodies to follow in my world. She told me that I must feel nothing. She took me under her wing and taught me everything Smooth taught her before me.

At first, she gave me small tasks like counting money. Next was learning how to tell good product from bad product, and learning the values. I was given my first pistol as a graduation gift when I graduated high school. That summer, I didn't do the things that most girls my age were doing. I wasn't preparing for college because that was the last thing on my mind. I practiced my aim all summer by shooting at still or moving targets. My mother also taught me to move silently by becoming one with the shadows. She said that a boss has control of her environment, and by becoming a part of it, she can never be caught slipping. Smooth's military training was instilled in my mother, making her the ultimate killing machine.

"Your daddy could have given me all his secret information he wanted to," my mother would tell me whenever I got frustrated with her teachings. "But if he hadn't worked me and taught me everything I'm teaching you, I would either be dead or on the arm of some motherfucka who could never hold a candle to your father. Understand? I'm not just teaching you how to run the business, Fire. I'm teaching you how to survive. You are a beautiful young woman, and you can get any man with your looks. But with what I'm instilling inside you, you can control them. Despite these goons we have patrolling around us wherever we go, realize you are your own army. They are just an extension of you. Remember that."

I replayed those words in my mind quite often. I thought of the last time I ever saw my mother alive . . .

*"Fire, if you leave and go anywhere today, let me know where you are going, and don't forget to wear your wig. You have a hair appointment for your sew-in tomorrow."*

*"OK, Mama," I replied as I sat at our huge dining room table, eating Cheerios and watching music videos. I glanced up at her and smirked.*

*She was dressed in a cream Burberry two-button pants suit with her hair pulled up on her head. Her accessories were minimal, just diamond square-cut earrings and her favorite diamond charm bracelet. It had a charm with the first letter of her name, my name, and Smooth's. Her shape resembled that of a pear, and her makeup was on point, as usual. My mother had seen millions and always walked out of the house looking like it.*

*Another day at the office, I thought to myself and ate the rest of my cereal.*

*"I love you, Mama," I told her when she grabbed her Burberry handbag off the marble counter. "When will you be home, or are you staying at the other house?"*

*She stopped in her tracks, turned, and came to where I sat at the table. She pulled me in her arms tight and kissed my forehead.*

*"I love you too, baby," she said and assured me she would be home. "I won't be too long. I just need to tie up a few loose ends with Jah. Close out a business deal."*

*"Jah? I don't like him, Mama," I told her like I always told her.*

*"You don't even know him, Fire," my mother said like always. "He was loyal to your daddy and is good to me."*

"All right, Mama, whatever. I'll see you later," I told her and blew her a kiss.

She caught it and pressed her balled fist to her chest.

"I love you, baby," she said again, and with that, she swished out of the kitchen and was gone.

When she left, I felt myself nod off at the table until Neffy woke me up, telling me it was time to go to the library. I got up from the table, ran to my room, threw on a yellow sundress, and put on some simple flip-flops. My driver, Paul, dropped me off at the library. He told me he would be back to get me in two hours, and as soon as he pulled off, I ran back outside to the street to the black Dodge Charger that had just pulled up.

"Hey, baby," I exclaimed once inside.

I hugged the boy I had secretly seen for the past few months. Tommy was sexy as hell, and he was a few years older than me. He was a typical dough boy, but he made good money. He was muscular with tattoos and curly hair pulled back into a ponytail with a baby face. I wouldn't say we were together. The only thing we did when we were together was having sex. That's all that I could make time for. He would try to take me on dates, but I could never sneak away for them. His eyes smiled at me before his mouth did.

"Wassup, babe?" he said and kissed me.

He drove away from the library, already knowing the drill. We talked briefly until he pulled into the empty parking garage for a company a few blocks from the library. As soon as the shadows shielded us, we went at each other. His lips met mine passionately, and our tongues explored each other's mouths. His hands fondled my breasts before pulling my dress down in the front and tenderly kissing my nipples. His tongue circled each nipple before he sucked and bit down on them, and a tingly feeling shot through my body down to where my pussy was purring.

"Mmm," I moaned, reaching for the bulge in his denim jeans. I unzipped them and pulled out his thick eight inches. Reaching into his pocket, I pulled out a condom he had there and slid it on for him. "Can I have it?"

As I asked him, I kicked off my flip-flops, leaned against the door, and opened my legs to him, revealing that I wasn't wearing any panties. I used my middle finger to circle my clit and touch my wetness. I was pleasing myself so well my head fell backward, and I relished the feeling. Tommy's answer was to lift me over the armrest and set me down on his dick. I moaned loudly as his dick rammed inside of me. He knew I liked it rough and didn't give me a chance to catch my breath before he began pounding upwardly. My vaginal walls were tight around his shaft, and my hands rested on his shoulders. My body was relaxed as he had his way with me. Tommy loved doing all the work.

"Sierra . . . fuck," Tommy said, burying his face in my neck. His large hands palmed my round behind while he used his muscles to bounce me up and down.

The car was rocking and filled with my squeals of pleasure. I felt my nut building up, and I began to grind into him until I couldn't take it anymore.

"Oooh, shiiit," I exclaimed as my body bucked. I threw my head back and felt his body jerking as well.

"Damn, baby," Tommy said, catching his breath, and we smiled at each other. "You have the best puss—"

He stopped midsentence with a look on his face like he was confused. His eyes were on my hair. My hands shot to my head, and I felt the wig was no longer there.

"Shit," I said and hoisted myself off him. I quickly grabbed the wig, placing it back on my head.

It was too late, however. He'd already seen that my hair was as red as fire.

"Can you take me back to the library, please?" I casually said like nothing had just happened.

Tommy just looked at me with the same funny look on his face. He didn't say anything, though. He did as I asked. When we pulled in front of the library, I saw that I still had a lot of time to kill, so I fixed myself and made sure my wig was in place. I didn't bother to kiss him farewell. I knew he was on funny time, and I was not in the mood for any questions.

"I'll see you later, Tommy," I told him. "I'll call you, OK?"

"A'ight," was all he said, and with that, I exited the vehicle and ran back into the library.

I thought it would be like any Thursday when I got home that evening. I took a shower and changed my clothes as soon as I arrived. I thought that I would chill out for the rest of the day, go out in the woods behind our house to practice my aim, and Neffy would make spaghetti like she did every Thursday. But when my mother came home that night, she didn't look at all like the way she left. I was upstairs in my room when I heard the doorbell ring, and shortly after, I heard Neffy's spine-chilling scream. I threw aside the book I was reading and jumped off my bed as fast as possible, worried about Neffy's well-being. I ran out of my room and down the stairs to the foyer, tripping over my own feet. When I reached her, I saw Neffy slowly backing away from the open front door with her hand clutching her heart. Her whole body was visibly trembling when I went and grabbed her shoulders.

"Neffy, what's wrong?" I asked, concerned, searching her face.

She didn't answer me; instead, she stared outside past the open front door at something on the stoop.

*I stepped slowly to the door to see what had shaken her up so badly. An unbearable odor crept into my nostrils before I saw the large cardboard box on the front stoop. The closer I got to the door, the stronger the smell got. The bottom of the box was soaked, and a red liquid was seeping onto the concrete stoop. My breathing slowed as I used one hand to cover my nose and reached the other to pull back one of the top flaps on the box. When I saw the contents of the box, my heart instantly stopped, and I screamed louder than Neffy had. What I stared at was a severed body, and on top was an arm . . . an arm with my mother's charm bracelet on it. I dropped to the ground and scooted back into the house as fast as possible, hysterical.*

*"No," I screamed. "No, no, no, no!"*

*My sobs filled the whole house. My mother was dead. She was inside the box. The liquid on the stoop was blood—my mother's blood. Neffy must have snapped to her senses because she ran and slammed the door shut. She then tried to get me off the ground, but I kept wriggling from her grasp, screaming and crying.*

*"We must go, Sierra!" she said urgently, calling me by my first name. "Hurry. We must go now!"*

*Everything was a blur to me. I felt like my heart had been ripped out and used as target practice. My whole body was numb. Neffy shoved three duffle bags in my arms and rushed me to the back, where a car was already waiting. She then hurried back into the house and returned holding a metal briefcase. When she finally got into the car, I smelled gasoline on her. I looked back at the house . . . into my home . . . and saw a fire growing inside it.*

*"Go, Paul," Neffy instructed our driver, who had been with us for years. "Get us far away from here."*

Three days later, I had made it my personal assignment to find out who was responsible for my mother's death. And I did. That was a week ago. I waited patiently and devised a plan for how I was going to kill each and every one of them.

# Chapter 2

My mom must have known that the way she lived would take her life one day. Long before she died, she gave Neffy access to all her accounts and all the information about her underground business. She even told her the name of the connect and how to contact him. She made Neffy take an oath to protect me no matter what, and that was exactly what she did. Neffy explained why she had to burn down my home and why we couldn't stay there. Nobody knew about that house, or so we had thought. If my mother's body was delivered there, Neffy realized they knew of the location and were making a statement. Neffy told me she didn't think anybody knew about me, but if they ran up in the house, they would clearly see three rooms being used, all our pictures, and she couldn't risk that.

I was lost. I had never been without my mother. The reality of the matter hadn't hit me yet. She always told me the day would come when she would be taken from me, and I would have to be strong just like she had to be when Smooth was killed. I just never assumed it would be so soon. Neffy handled business. Within two days, we had another roof over our heads, tucked off in the suburbs with furniture and new wardrobes.

When I brought up the other house my mother stayed in, she told me that was where my mom kept all her work.

In the basement was a cellar with a trap door. Neffy said that only me, my mother, and my father could open it. The morning I saw my mother, she said she had some business to attend to. I assumed that she had re-upped. But even the mention of going to that house was out of the question to Neffy. She almost had a heart attack the day I decided I was going. I was already dressed in an all-black hoodie and cargos, ready to go. I had my hair pulled back with a bandanna and wore running shoes. The only thing I didn't have was my pistol, and I regretted not grabbing it from my room. I wasn't too upset, however. Getting a throwaway in the streets was nothing.

"Hell no! So whoever got your mother can get you too?" Neffy said to me on our third night in the new house. She waved her hands in the air. "No. Absolutely not. I promised your mother—"

"I know what you promised her," I exclaimed, sitting on our new couch. "But I have to go to that house. It's been two days since she—People know, the streets talk, and I know people are getting in position to take her place already. I'm going, and there is nothing you can do to stop me. You're not my mother, Neffy."

Neffy stared at me for a moment. She sat before me in jeans and a T-shir, looking like she didn't know what to say. Her long hair was down, making her chocolate face look like a heart. Her full lips were pursed, and her almond-brown eyes looked lost. What she didn't know was that I had already made up my mind. I didn't have any more guidance. I was going based on instinct. I was going to the house, and it would be only my second trip there. My first was earlier that day when I cased the place.

The way Neffy stared back at me, I knew she understood there was no stopping me. She stood up and left the small country-style living room for a few minutes. When she returned, she had the same metal briefcase she'd had when she exited our old house. She sat on the couch across from me and slid the briefcase across the table. She said nothing; she didn't need to. I grabbed the briefcase by the handle, pulling it closer to me. When I opened it, I saw two things that meant the world to me: my pistol and my mother's bracelet.

Neffy had to have gotten the bracelet from my mother's severed arm, I knew that was probably a hard task, but I was very thankful at that moment for her. Suddenly, the thought of my mother's body in that cardboard box burning down with our home was too much to bear. Instantly, I shook the thought out of my head. I refused to think about it. I placed the bracelet on my arm and went over to the couch to hug Neffy tight. When we broke our embrace, she kissed my cheek.

"Paul will take you," she told me. "Tell him to make sure he uses the back streets. Be careful, Sierra. You are like your mother in many ways. Being fearless is a strength, but it was also her biggest weakness."

With that, she left the living room, leaving me by myself. When she was gone, I grabbed my pistol, checked the clip, and left. I was determined to get to where I knew I needed to be. Paul was already in the front of the house, waiting for me. Walking down the sidewalk toward the street where the Maybach was parked, I felt a pair of eyes on me. I turned my head just in time to see a boy around my age sitting on the porch of the house next to the one Neffy and I were staying in. He was dressed casually in jeans and a white T-shirt with a black Nike sign. On his feet he wore Nike flip-flops and high Nike ankle socks.

"Damn, girl," he said, smiling and showing off his all-white perfect smile. "Who you finna go at?"

I rolled my eyes at him. Dude was beyond handsome, I would give him that. His waves were so deep I could get seasick, but right then was definitely not the time to try to speak to me.

"You, if you don't shut the fuck up talking to me," I told him and glared at him. Then I kept walking.

I had reached the car by then. Paul opened my door, and I climbed in the back.

"If the boys come looking for you, I got you. I ain't see *nothin'*," the boy joked, and I gave him the middle finger.

"Bitch," I said under my breath.

Paul got into the car and pulled off.

The Maybach's tinted windows shielded me from the boy's continued stare, but I paid him no mind. I was only focused on the task at hand. Next to me was a duffle bag I would need to stuff the cocaine in.

*In and out,* I thought to myself.

Although my mother's job in life was to keep me a secret and introduce me to the world when the time was right, I don't think she understood that no time would ever be right. There would always be a hungry nigga trying to come up. She learned the hard way. Paul pulled slowly into the neighborhood on the next block from the house.

"I'm letting you out here," he said, looking straight ahead. I stared at his balding head. "And, Sierra?"

"Yes, Paul?" I asked.

"Be careful."

I understood then why Paul didn't look back at me. He might not have let me out of the car if he did. But he was loyal to my mother and knew that her work couldn't die with her. I leaned up and kissed him on his cheek.

"I'm an orphan, Paul. My mother is dead. I never knew my father. Even if I didn't want to do this, I would. It's all I know."

Paul nodded his head slowly and handed me a set of keys."These will get you into every locked room in the house," he said as I took the keys.

I pulled a black face mask over my face and instead of responding, I checked the clip to my gun again and, without another word, I got out of the vehicle with the duffle bag slung over my shoulder and sprinted toward the house. All the homes were large, and, even in the dark, I could tell they were beautiful. I was thankful the house was in Hyde Park. I didn't have to worry about anyone being outside that time of night.

It didn't take long for me to get to the big white house, and when I did, I saw the black Chevy Tahoe parked a few houses down. I checked my surroundings before sprinting to the back of the house, moving in the shadows. I used one of the keys Paul gave me to open the back door and quickly shut it behind me.

My mother's scent invaded my nostrils, and my legs threatened to give way under me. My stomach filled with knots as I remembered seeing her severed body in the box. I shook the thought from my head because I knew I had to finish what I set out to do. I hadn't allowed myself to mourn my mother just because a part of me was still in denial.

I forced myself to remember Neffy's instructions and used them to guide me through the house, using my flashlight and keeping my gun raised. I was careful not to look at or touch anything until I reached the kitchen and spotted the door Neffy said led to the cellar. I used another of the keys Paul gave me to unlock that door and cautiously walked down the stairs. Once my feet were planted on the cellar floor, I flashed my light on the wall to my right in search of the light switch.

I flipped the switch and lit up the entire cellar. "Now, where the fuck is this door?" I said to myself, setting my gun and flashlight down.

The cellar had a bar and was filled with bottles of wine. I smiled because I knew this wasn't my mother's forte. Smooth had taste. Everything, including the bar, was made of fine marble, and the walls were filled with pictures of him with my mother. My eyes fell on a life-size picture hanging on the wall, separated by every other photo. It was a picture of my father by himself. He stood next to a Lexus dressed in a suit with a smile plastered on his face. One hand was in his suit pants pocket, and the other was up like he was waving at somebody. He was handsome, and my mother was right. I was the spitting image of him. His hair was just as red as mine, and the freckles on his light skin were the mirror image of my own. The only difference was our eyes. I had my mother's hazel eyes.

I smiled at the picture, suddenly forgetting why I was in the cellar in the first place. I walked up to the tall picture until I was eye to eye with Smooth. I never knew him, but I felt closer to him at that moment like I'd known him. I was him. Without thinking, my hand raised and pressed where his hand was in the picture. I imagined what it would feel like if our palms touched, and just as I was about to withdraw my hand, I felt warmth beneath it and heard a click behind the picture. Instinct made me jump back as the wall behind the picture suddenly opened like a door. The hidden door.

Instead of standing there dumbfounded, I pushed the door open more and stepped through it. What I saw took my breath away. I was now in an artillery room. Weapons were hung up and covered all four walls. The room wasn't very large, but it was big enough. In the center stood a table, and on it, at least 200 bricks of pure cocaine. My duffle bag was big, but it wasn't big enough to take it all. It could probably fit fifty in it. I didn't want to leave anything behind, so I put it upon myself to make four trips to and from the truck. Risky, but I refused to leave any behind. I even planned to take some of the guns and explosives that caught my attention on the wall.

Everything was going without a hitch, but on the last trip, I began to bag the last of the product when I suddenly heard footsteps above me. I paused to make sure I wasn't going out of my mind, but then I began hearing voices.

"Fuck," I said aloud and zipped up the bag.

I slung it over my shoulder and shut the hidden door, not knowing when I would need to visit it again. I figured they were robbers who noticed the house had been un-tended for a few days. I didn't care to preserve anything in the place just because it meant nothing to me. I was quiet as I listened to the voices upstairs. I could tell they were in the kitchen by how well I could make out their words. I went and grabbed my gun and flashlight from where I'd set them down and proceeded to go through the window in the cellar to get to the truck.

"Jah!" I heard a man's muffled voice say, and I stopped in my tracks. "Where you think this bitch kept it at?"

*Jah?* I thought to myself.

"I don't know, Smoke," I heard another man's voice say. "But I know it's in this house. The way Smooth and Chleo used to keep this muhfucka guarded, I know it's here."

"I still can't believe Lou hacked that bitch to pieces, and she still ain't sing," the other voice spoke again as I heard them moving around the house.

"Well," Jah said, "she was a little too much like her dead husband—stupid muhfuckas. I think I let her live a little too long. I should have had her killed the same night Smooth died. This shit has dragged on for years. I had to play my cards right, but don't trip. Chleo never told me when she copped. I just knew she had it. But this time, she let it slip that she had just re-upped. I knew then that it was time for Chicago to see a king again. She was too soft in the streets. If it wasn't me, it would have been somebody else."

More words were spoken, but my blood was boiling. Jah killed my mother? Jah was Smooth's right-hand man. My mother constantly spoke of his loyalty to her. But it made sense now. Smooth didn't tell him the information that he told my mother. I understood why. He'd set my father up, and now, he'd killed my mother. I dropped the flashlight in my hands and began making my way up the stairs, prepared to kill Jah and the other man whose voice I heard. But before I could open the door, I heard several more footsteps and more muffled voices. Jah was barking out instructions to what seemed like a small army, and I knew I couldn't do much. I was positive every man in the room was armed. I weighed my options and decided now wasn't the time to wage war. I'd die. Instead, I bounded back down the stairs.

"That's the door to the cellar. Shoot that muhfucka open," I heard Jah say when I was halfway back down the stairs.

I didn't skip a beat. My footsteps were loud as I ran down the remaining stairs.

"Jah . . . Jah, I think somebody is down there!"

*Go,* I willed myself.

As they shot at the door leading to the cellar, I shot out the window leading me out of the house. I threw the huge duffle bag out the window, and just as I heard the footsteps bounding down the stairs, I hoisted myself through the window.

"Shoot them!" I heard somebody shout behind me, but I was already gone and in a sprint to where Paul was parked a little ways away, waiting for me.

# Chapter 3

Once I was inside the vehicle, Paul sped off. My heart was racing, and I kept looking behind me in paranoia, hoping nobody had followed me. We drove back to the new house without stopping. When I got to the house, it had to be almost two o'clock in the morning. The neighborhood was still, and nobody was outside, although a few lights were on. We pulled into the driveway and noticed Neffy's light was still on, and I knew it was because she was waiting on me to get home safely. I needed some fresh air and time to take in my newfound knowledge. I rolled down my window and sat there for almost five minutes before deciding to move the product into the house.

Paul opened my door and let me out, and just as I was about to start walking, I saw a shadowy figure approaching me. My instinct was to grab my gun and aim it.

"Whoa!" I saw the boy from across the street standing beside the car with his hands up. "I just saw y'all sitting here for a long time. I was just coming to make sure you were straight."

The look on his face was sincere, but I still took my sweet time lowering my gun. I looked at Paul, who looked ready to shoot the dude himself, and let him know it was okay. He nodded and got back inside of the car to back it up to the garage. The boy's eyes traveled to the bag I held, and his eyes got big.

"Yo, what the fuck?" he said. "You some type of queen pin or something?"

I didn't respond. Instead, I went to press the code to open the garage.

"You need help?" the boy said, and I just stared at him.

"No thanks," I said bitterly.

I contemplated whether I should let him live as I began unloading the car. He'd seen too much; he was a liability. When I was finished, I turned back to him.

"I knew you were leaving on some gangster shit," the boy continued. "Now I guess you either have to kill me . . . or cut me in. That has to be at least a million dollars' worth of bricks right there."

"Glad to know you know your math." I glared at him with my trigger finger itching.

He saw my finger move and shook his head, placing his hand on his brush cut.

"So, since you gon' kill a nigga anyway, just do me a favor and set my grandma up real nice. I've caused her enough trouble in my 26 years of life," he told me, accepting his fate. "But before you pull that trigger, I think I have a right to know who's taking my life."

I studied his physique and stared at the determined look on his face. I didn't know him from a can of paint, but something told me to trust him.

"What's your name?"

"Calvin," he answered.

"Well, Calvin, my name is Sierra Thompson, daughter of Chleo and Smooth Thompson. Everyone calls me Fire because of my hair."

Calvin's eyes got big and instantly shot to my red hair.

"Ain't that about a bitch," he said, shaking his head again. "You look just like that nigga."

"You knew him?"

"No, but he did some business with my uncle back in the day. If Chleo is your mother, what you doing in a neighborhood like this? She runs the streets. Why aren't you in a mansion somewhere?"

"She's dead," I said, shutting the back door of the truck and turning to face him again. I didn't know why I was telling him everything, but some part of me felt the need to say it aloud. "She was murdered three days ago, and her body was delivered hacked into pieces at my front door. The niggas who did it were at the place where I had to grab this shit from. Trying to get it for themselves . . . It was my father's partner. His best friend. He was also my mother's business partner when my father was murdered. I found out tonight he was behind both deaths. Now I'm alone. The only thing my mother taught me how to do is kill. She never got around to showing me how to run an empire. So I'm stuck with $4 million worth of cocaine, and I'm supposed to continue my parents' legacy . . . but all I can think about is killing the nigga responsible for it all. Jah."

Calvin was quiet. He just stood and stared intently into my eyes with his dark brown ones, and his chocolate brown skin glistened in the night. I couldn't read the expression on his face, but what he said next shocked me.

"Let's kill him," he finally said in all seriousness.

"What?" I asked, looking dumbfounded.

"If I help you kill him, then you let me live and get in on everything you have going on. My uncle knew your father. He lives in New York right now and, to your luck, is looking for a new connect. By one look at you, he'll know you're legit. Only thing is, I won't give you any of his information until you give me your word."

I laughed. "You don't know me. Why would you help me? You could be setting me up. How do I know that putting a bullet in your head won't be a lot safer for me?"

"I don't have to. A little behind-the-scenes from me. A few years ago, I was a little heavy in the streets, making my money how I knew how. A nigga stepped to me, and I killed him. But I was acquitted of the murder charge, and my grandmother went broke paying my lawyers. Your mother looked out for us. You see, my grandmother was known in our hood. She used to feed the whole block. Your mother was notorious for stopping by to grab a plate of my mother's spicy greens. She bought my grandmother this house just off GP when we got evicted. Chleo had a good heart. You are just giving me a chance to pay back an old debt. Plus, if I want in on this shit here, I have to prove my loyalty somehow. Feel me?"

I stared at him, trying to determine whether he was telling the truth. When I saw no lies, I nodded my head.

"Come in," I finally said, and Calvin followed me inside the house after I shut the garage door.

"If you don't mind me asking," Calvin said once we were in the living room, "why didn't anybody know that Smooth and Chleo had a daughter? You should be the princess of the streets right now."

"For my protection," I said, sitting across from him. "And now I know why I needed to be protected. "

I broke down my whole story . . . my birth all the way to the present. I told him I refused to mourn my mother until she was avenged. Everything was happening too fast for me, but I knew what I needed to do. I had the resources to do it all. I just needed the right setup. I knew at that moment Jah was feeling it. He had no idea who had gotten to the house before him, and I was sure he had the streets being swept. That was right where I wanted him. I just needed to figure out how I would be able to touch him. I was sure everyone loyal to my mother was now Team Jah, so I knew his security would be highly enforced now that I'd gotten to the cocaine first. I told Calvin that I didn't give a fuck about that, though.

For the rest of the night, he and I devised a plan. We had to make sure there were no loose ends. After a few hours with Calvin, I didn't find it odd that he had just met me and now was helping me plot out a murder. He was just a young nigga looking for a come-up, and in me, he'd found one.

# Chapter 4

Our plan was foolproof. I had complete confidence that it would work. Calvin and I took one more day to ensure all loose ends were tied. Since we both knew that Jah was looking for a connect, Calvin's role was to pretend to be that. We took him shopping to look at the part, and then he would make contact. Neffy had been in the family since before I was born, so she could tell me all Jah's common spots. The only thing she didn't know was where he laid his head. But the information she gave us was sufficient.

Calvin's face was known in the streets of Chicago from his past of moving weight, so when he walked up to Jah in his favorite bar, he could step to him without a problem. Calvin's story was that his uncle in New York was thinking about expanding to Chicago, and he needed somebody there to partner with. Jah knew who Calvin's uncle was, and to make matters even better, Calvin had some product for Jah to sample. Calvin threw Jah some powder and the deal, and since he was thirsty to get some new work, Jah jumped at the opportunity. They set up a time that night to meet and make the transaction.

When Calvin told me the story, I couldn't believe how easy and fast it was all going down. We were sitting in the basement of my house, getting everything ready for the transaction. The past few days, I made Calvin stay at my place in the basement. That way, I could be sure he didn't try to do any funny shit. I didn't think he would, but I still had to be cautious.

"Be careful, Calvin," Neffy said. "I always felt that Jah was a snake, and now I know I was right. He's the type of man to want the world without paying for it."

Since we moved into the neighborhood, Neffy had taken a particular liking to Calvin. She liked his sense of business savvy and how he had turned it into a business venture instead of robbing me.

"That's where I come in at, Nef," I said while shining my gun. "One-woman army."

"Fire—" Neffy started, and by the tone of her voice, I already knew what was coming next.

"It's too late, Nef," I told her. "I'm in too deep. I can't sleep at night knowing the man who killed my mother is still breathing, knowing that the people she fed already forgot about her and just moved on to the next nigga. I can't."

"I was just going to say"—Neffy came and hugged me— "I've been around for a long time. Working for your mother and father, I've seen a lot. But just know that your bloodline is like royalty in the streets of Chicago. Ever wonder why they took so well to a woman queen pin after Smooth was killed? No, they were not bound by blood, but she was created in his image. He made her who she was, just like she made you who you are. Do not be angry at the people, baby. Their loyalty is only in limbo because you are. Think about that one. I love you."

When she was gone, I looked at Calvin, who was loading the chrome 9 mm pistol I'd given him and preparing to place it in the waist of his Armani slacks. His hair was freshly cut, and his strong jawline was clenched. The expression on his face spelled one word: *determination*. He grabbed the jacket to his suit from one of the tables in the small basement and put it on.

"You know you might die tonight, right?" I asked. "I might die too. You sure you want to ride this out with me?"

Calvin finished buttoning his suit jacket and smoothed it down. He stood before me, not looking like the thug he had when I first laid eyes on him. He stood before me, looking like a boss. He took his time with his response.

"I always watched movies . . . when niggas meet a bitch and randomly come up with her. When I was out there handling my business, the most I ever saw was five hundred thousand. I'm trying to see my first million. I never thought that shit could be real life. When I first saw you, I had plans to come at you, but I didn't know how. You got this aura about you that women older than you would admire. Of course, there is a possibility that we will die, ma. But honestly, I don't have much to live for right now. However, there also is that possibility that we won't. And if we don't, that means a future with a lot of money and a beautiful woman by my side. I'll take my chances."

I squinted my eyes at him. "All this to get some pussy?"

"All this to build an empire," Calvin said. "Now, get ready. It's almost time for the show to start."

Jah had instructed Calvin to meet him at a construction site after all the workers left. Paul drove Calvin to the site to give the illusion of a boss, and I wasn't too far behind them. I parked the Tahoe some distance from them and footed the rest of the way. Once again, I was dressed in all black. This time, however, I didn't wear a face mask. Instead, I pulled my long red hair back into a black bandanna. I wore a black jumpsuit and black combat boots. I had an artillery belt on my waist and all-black gloves on my hands. As I ran toward where I heard voices, I darted from shadow to shadow. When I finally reached them, I kept my distance and held my gun.

I didn't have a good shot at Jah. Calvin was in the way, but I knew all I had to do was wait for the perfect opportunity. The two men stood in the only lit-up spot of the construction site, and behind Jah stood a small army. No one was behind Calvin, only the three duffle bags beside him. If he was nervous, he definitely didn't show it.

"You came alone?" I heard Jah say to Calvin, and I heard Calvin chuckle in response.

"I've heard enough about you in these streets to know better than to come alone," Calvin bluffed.

I saw Jah cautiously look around, so I moved behind a tractor to avoid being seen.

"Smart man," Jah said.

I studied him. I'd seen him in pictures, but seeing him in person was completely different. His skin was fair, and he looked only five foot eight. His mustache went into his freshly trimmed beard, making his face look even more menacing. His eyes were cold and unfeeling, and his bushy eyebrows were furrowed like he was standing there before Calvin in deep thought. One glance and I didn't peg him as a businessman. He was still wearing street clothes. He was just a common street thug who'd lucked up. I felt the anger inside of me boiling, and it took everything in me not to shoot him.

"This is a business meeting, correct?" Calvin asked, motioning toward the bags. "I would honestly like to make this quick. Usually, when I do business with people, there is less talk and more hustle."

Jah looked at Calvin and then behind him at the men standing there. He suddenly burst into laughter.

"It's funny that you say that," Jah said, pacing back and forth. He wagged a finger in Calvin's direction. "Because when I do this kind of business with people, I usually get my facts first. You see, I know your uncle Los. I've known him for a while now . . . and there is one thing I know about that nigga. He *never* throws deals on his produce. Los is a 'what you see is what you get' type of nigga, so when you were offering his product so low, I decided to reach out to the nigga and see what was up . . . just because some shit ain't smell right, you feeling me? And what do you know? This nigga didn't know about any of this shit. Also, I had niggas here waiting before anybody pulled up, so I know you came alone."

Everything was falling apart right before my eyes. I'd sent Calvin on a suicide mission and saw his hand twitch toward his gun. I cocked mine as well.

"And another funny thing." Jah continued to chuckle to himself. "The other night, one of my houses got hit. The nigga got away with almost $2 million of cocaine. Now, tell me." Jah pulled his gun out, and the men behind him did the same. "Where is the rest of it? Because it seems that you tryin'a sell me something that's already mine."

I had to make my move. I grabbed a grenade from my artillery belt, pulled the pin, and threw it behind Jah at his entourage. The explosion knocked all five men off their feet and immediately made my presence known while they were down.

"Who would ever come alone to a business meeting with a snake like you?" I asked with my gun pointed at Jah.

Jah turned around and saw all his men disabled. He then turned back to us. He put his hands up when he saw Calvin's gun and my gun pointed at him.

"Who the fuck are ya? Bonnie and Clyde? Robbing me for fifty thousand? That's chump change. Y'all can have it and keep the product." Jah tried to reason with us.

"If what? We let you live?" I said, laughing. "This isn't about the product or the money, you stupid nigga. I have an old score to settle with you."

I saw one of the men behind Jah try to get up, so I sent a hollow tip through his head. My gunshot echoed through the whole site. Half his head was blown off, and the blood and brains splattered on the others lying near him.

"Stay down," I barked at the rest of them. I walked into the light and stood next to Calvin so Jah could better look at me.

"Recognize me?" I asked.

"I've never seen you in my life." Jah glared at me. "I don't know who the fuck you are."

"You knew my father," I told him.

"Wh–" Before the question had fully formed, I removed the bandanna from my head. My red hair fell loosely on my shoulders. The look on his face was priceless, and I drank in his expression.

"There it is," I said.

"Smooth?" Jah asked in shock.

"Yes . . . I'm his daughter. And Chleo was my mother," I told him. "You killed both of them behind your greed, and now, I'm going to kill you and sit rightfully in the spot you are trying to take."

Just as I was about to pull my trigger, I heard a gunshot and felt Calvin go down beside me. I had been so busy talking to Jah that I hadn't noticed one of the men behind him grab their gun. Caught off guard, I took my eyes off Jah, which proved to be the biggest mistake of my life. He rushed me to the ground and got the gun out of my hands. He hit me in the face with the butt of the weapon, and I felt a bone in my face crack.

"Bitch!" Jah exclaimed and stood up next to me. He kicked me as hard as he could in my ribs.

I cried out and saw Calvin out of the corner of my eyes, trying to get to me as Jah towered over me with his gun pointed at my head. "Did you *really* think you were going to stop me? I killed the biggest in the city, and now, I will do the same to you. Then guess what I'ma do . . . clean this shit up like it never even happened. Any last words?"

I struggled to catch my breath as I lay there, feeling like I was dying. "Bitch," I coughed right before one shot rang . . . and I felt nothing . . .


"Sierra, Sierra, wake up!" I felt somebody shaking me, and I jumped up.

"Wha-what?" I asked, frantically searching my body. "Where am I?"

I looked around and saw that I was in my old house, seated at the dining room table with a bowl of cereal in front of me. Neffy was standing over me with a bewildered look on her face.

"You're at home, baby. Paul is here to take you to the library," she said, like I was being ridiculous.

"Library . . . What?" I was confused. Then I suddenly remembered something. "Mama! Where's my mom, Neffy?"

"She just left." Neffy was looking at me like I was crazy at that point. "You just said bye to her. Sierra, honey, are you feeling OK?"

"No!" I screamed and jumped up. I was preparing to run to the door to go after her, but the front door opened just as I got to the foyer.

"I forgot something." My mother's voice rang out as she took her first step into the house.

Before she could shut the door, my arms were around her neck, and I sobbed.

"Stay!" I said over and over in her neck.

My mother looked at Neffy with confusion plastered on her face. Neffy just shrugged her shoulders. My mother stood back and looked at my face. I couldn't get out what was wrong with me, but my mother knew something happening.

"Please stay," I cried out again.

"OK," my mother said to me. "OK, baby. I'll make a few phone calls and stay home with you. All right?"

I nodded and clung to my mother, not wanting to lose her again. I didn't know if my dream would come true, but I refused to take my chances. That moment right there meant the world to me, and my mother would never know it. She was all I had, and that was one thing I understood about the dream. If she died, the streets would have to mourn two deaths because I would die too. But that was something I was going to make sure never happened.

# *Greed*

by

*Marcus Weber*

# Chapter 1

"Death is only the beginning," an unforgiving voice spoke softly.

Five men stood around another man tied to a chair in the middle of a garage. The light directly above them shone dimly, accenting the grim scene. The man attached to the wooden chair sat quivering, looking hopeless. He had already tried to plead his innocence, but his words fell on uncaring ears. He looked into the eyes of the muscular figure before him and realized that he was staring at the Grim Reaper himself.

Denny Capello stood directly in front of the terrified man with murder in his eyes. The only thing separating the two of them was a table. On top of that table were two items: a syringe and a metal bat.

"I trusted you, Chris," Denny spoke again. "You're my cousin, but I loved you like a brother. Why would you steal from my office? You must have thought that taking the security footage from my home would cover your tracks."

Denny had never felt more betrayed in his life. Not only was he missing $150,000 from his home safe, but the offender was none other than his own flesh and blood. One of his most trusted workers informed him that he saw Chris take the money. Shortly after, Chris left town for a few days, and Denny didn't hear from him.

As Denny spoke, he grabbed the syringe and thumped the needle. Chris, whose mouth was duct taped shut, tried to scream, but the sound was muffled. Seeing the murder in Denny's eyes, Chris fought hard against his restraints and made silent pleas with his eyes. Denny laughed out loud at the sounds Chris was making.

"Whose idea was the duct tape?" he asked with his thick Spanish accent. He looked around at the circle of men, and his eyes fell on Diablo, who had come forth with the news of the betrayal. He nodded his approval. "Good job. Can't have all of New York hearing the cries of this scum, can we?" Denny said, thumping the needle with his finger. "You have been working with me for years, Chris—years. Not only are you my blood, but you are also my lieutenant. You have seen firsthand what happens to those who betray my trust. You have assisted with it. You are the only person who knew the combination to the safe, and Diablo here says he saw you taking the money from my safe out in a suitcase."

Chris's eyes opened even wider, and he whipped his head to face Diablo, who looked away. His brow furrowed, and he shook his head, trying to plead his case, but the duct tape over his mouth prevented his speech. He fought so hard against the ropes around his arms and ankles that the chair shook back and forth. Finally, Chris gave up, knowing that fighting was no use. There was no point in fighting for his innocence because Denny was far past the point of reason.

"This, my dear cousin"—Denny nodded his head toward the needle in his hand and spoke so icily that he once again demanded Chris's attention—"is rat poison. I want you to witness and feel every horrific thing I'm about to do to your body."

Without warning, Denny reached over the table, jabbed the needle into Chris's neck, and released the poison into his body. It didn't take too long for Chris to start feeling the effects of it coursing through his veins. He began to lose the ability to move his body parts. Within minutes, the only things Chris could move were his eyes. Next, Denny set down the syringe to grab the bat. His anger got the best of him, and he kicked the table between them out of the way to get in Chris's face.

"Did you think I wouldn't discover that you've been stealing from me for years? After Diablo brought this shit to my attention, I had my accountant check all my numbers, and lo and behold, it turns out that almost half a million dollars have gone missing from right under my nose. I never questioned giving you any of the codes to any of my safes or access to any of my bank accounts because I trusted you. We were raised like brothers."

Denny brought the bat down on Chris's knee so hard that everyone in the garage heard the bone crack upon impact. Chris had no choice but to stomach the pain. He clenched his eyes shut, and a pained groan erupted from his throat. When he opened his eyes, tears spilled from them, and they fell on his injured leg. Denny hit the broken bone again with just as much force, and Chris screamed like a tortured animal through his sealed lips and tried to catch his breath. Denny backed away and went to one of the shelves in the garage, the one with all the tools. Chris used that time to gather his wits and glare again at Diablo in disbelief. His chest was heaving, and he wanted nothing more than to pass out, but he knew how his cousin operated. His torture had just begun.

He could take another breath just before he heard the sound of chains dragging on the ground. He looked up in time to see the metal chain being hurdled toward his face right before he felt the pain.

Unknown to the men in the garage, their every move was being watched by a pair of tiny eyes. Nine-year-old Taina Capello stared at the brutal act her father was performing from behind a tall trash bin. Her lip shook, and she bit down to keep her whimper from coming up. Earlier, she had been asleep for a while before she had heard suspicious sounds coming from the garage of their raised-ranch-style, five-bedroom home. It hadn't been the first time her father had used his garage as a torture chamber, but that night, something made her get up from the bed. Her mother would have a fit if she knew that her baby girl was sneaking around, spying. That was why Taina knew she must be as silent and quick as possible. She swore that her mother had eyes in the back of her head and bionic hearing.

Taina wrapped the silk robe her grandmother gifted her on her last birthday around her petite body and hurried out of her room. When she passed her parents' bedroom, she peeked in to see what her mother was doing but quickly saw that she was fast asleep and had plugs positioned snugly in her ears. Taina knew what that meant. Whenever her father thought it might get a little noisy at night, he told her mother to wear them to sleep. Knowing that the coast was clear, Taina walked fast through the house until she got to the spacious kitchen of their home. The door leading to the garage was open just a slit—enough for her to slide through the opening without touching it or being seen.

She ducked down and got on all fours to crawl behind the family's tall black trash bin. The horrible smell suddenly reminded her that she was supposed to take it to the curb. The trashmen would be there in the wee hours of the morning. Taina made a mental note to do that before her mother found out she had forgotten to do one of her chores.

Taina heard her father speaking to her cousin, Chris, and her heart beat fast at the accusations she heard directed at him. She peeked around the bin to look at the gruesome scene beginning to unravel and looked helplessly at Chris, who she loved dearly, almost as much as she loved her father.

"Stop, Papi," Taina whispered to herself, trying to will her father to stop the attack, but he did the exact opposite.

Taina put her shaking fingers to her mouth, trying to decide what to do. She knew that if she made her presence known, she would be in big trouble with her father. But he needed to know that the man who had betrayed his trust was indeed in the garage, but it was not the man who he had strapped to the chair.

Taina knew for a fact that it was not Chris who had stolen Denny's money from the safe in his office. She remembered the day perfectly.

One of the neighboring parents had dropped her off early from soccer practice, and nobody important was home yet, only the maids. They were doing what they always did when they thought nobody was home, standing in the backyard smoking marijuana. Taina was thrilled to have the house to herself. That meant she could sneak some ice cream and watch an R-rated movie before her parents arrived home. As she was sitting in front of the sixty-inch floor television in the family room of the home her father had built from the ground up, she heard footsteps coming from upstairs.

Taina had never been the type to run from danger. She was the type of kid to check out what was happening.

Standing up, she set her almost-empty bowl of cookies and cream to the side and wiped her hands on her soccer shorts. Walking to the stairs, she slowly crept up them and stretched her neck to see who was cutting into her time. When she finally reached the second level, the noises got louder and more distinct. They came from her father's office, and Taina knew her father wasn't there. She also knew that nobody was allowed in her father's office—only her cousin, who she viewed more as an uncle.

"Cousin Chris?" Taina's high-pitched voice called, assuming that it was him.

She pushed the door open to see who was in the office, but as she pushed, someone pulled. Taina was shocked at the face she saw on the other end of the door. It wasn't her father or Chris. It was another one of Denny's trusted hands, Diablo. Taina looked at him with a confused look frozen on her young and innocent face. He looked just as shocked to see her as she was to see him, but he quickly recovered.

"*Lo siento mucho*. I'm so sorry, princess." He flashed her a charming smile. "I did not know anyone would be home."

"What are you doing in my papi's office?" Taina asked, her eyes finally landing on the black bag hanging from Diablo's shoulder. It was slightly open, and she could peer inside and see what was there. Her eyes widened.

Diablo noticed her alarm and thought fast.

"Your father and I were out in the . . . um,"—he cleared his throat—"in the field, and he needed me to run here and grab a few things for him. His hands are tied up at the moment. We all know how busy your father gets." He gave a small laugh.

"He's waiting for me, and I don't want to keep him waiting." He stepped out of the office and shut the locked door before Taina could look at what was behind him. However, she noticed that he had a small disk in his hand. "Would you like me to tell him you are home alone?"

Taina quickly forgot her suspicions and shook her head fast. "No, that's OK," she said. "My mom should be home soon."

With that, Diablo planted a kiss on her forehead, walked past her to the steps, and headed for the front door.

"See you at dinner on Sunday, princess," he called to her over his shoulder right before the door slammed shut.

After that, Taina put the incident to the back of her mind, but that night, as she perched behind the stinky trash, the images of Diablo leaving Denny's office with a bag full of cash just didn't add up. Taina felt tears falling down her pretty face when she saw how helpless her cousin was. She understood why Diablo stood there looking like he had won the lottery, and she also knew why he had given her father the idea to tape his mouth shut. It wasn't so that New York couldn't hear his cries. It was so that he wouldn't tell who the culprit really was. Taina watched her father hit Chris a few more times, but soon, the spreading blood became too much for her to bear.

"Papi!" she yelled and jumped up from behind the trash can in the corner. "Stop it!"

Denny was so shocked to hear Taina's voice that he stopped his attack on Chris's face. Turning his head, he saw his beautiful baby girl standing behind him with tears on her face . . . the face that mirrored his exactly. The men surrounding Chris didn't miss a beat. They stood in front of Chris, hoping to shield her eyes from seeing the shape that he was in, but it was too late. She had already seen enough, and the horrified look in her eyes told Denny just that.

"Taina," Denny said, shaking his head. "What are you doing out of bed, sweetheart?"

"I heard noises," she said. "I heard screams. I—Oh, Papi, what are you doing to Chris?"

Denny turned his head back to Chris, whose head was nodding as he tried to stay conscious. He could lie to his child all he wanted, but unlike most kids her age, Taina wasn't stupid.

"This is what happens to anyone who betrays your father," he told her. "Cousin Chris has been a very bad man, baby. And now he must pay the cost. But you know you are not supposed to be out of bed once it is bedtime. Take her back to her room." He motioned for one of the men to escort Taina back to her bedroom.

Taina backed away from the advancing man, and her bare foot stepped into something cold and wet. She looked down and saw that she was standing in a small puddle of blood on the concrete floor. She knew that her innocent cousin would die if she didn't speak.

"Papi, it wasn't cousin Chris." Taina looked up and glared at Diablo, who looked like he had just seen a ghost.

"Somebody get her to bed," Diablo said, hoping one of the men would listen. "Now!"

Taina snatched away from her father's henchmen.

"It wasn't Chris, Papi!" She started sobbing uncontrollably. "The other day, Mrs. Sanchez dropped me off early from soccer practice, and I saw Diablo coming from your office with a bag of money, Papi. You have to believe me."

Taina ran past the men to a bloody Chris and stood with her hands wide. "You can't hurt him anymore!" she screamed. "I won't let you!"

Denny stood there in pure shock and pulled his pistol from his waist. The murderous stare that had once been on Chris was now targeted at Diablo.

"Is this true?"

Diablo's voice betrayed him when he tried to answer, and nothing came out. His plan had just folded right before his eyes, and he knew the cat was out of the bag. He didn't know what to say.

"Boss, I—" he started, but Denny silenced that with one shot to his knee.

Diablo instantly dropped to the ground, crying in pain. The pain from the bullet and the impact from the fall knocked the wind out of him, and he rolled over on his back, trying to nurse his knee.

"So you would have me kill my own blood in rage?" Denny's voice was lethal. "Behind your treacherous acts of betrayal?"

Denny shot Diablo's other knee, and his screams caused Taina to jump. Seeing this, Denny went to Diablo and kicked him in his face.

"Shut the fuck up," he said. "You are scaring my daughter. Get this son of a bitch out of here. Hog-tie him to the heaviest weight you can find and throw him into a river."

"And his family, boss?"

"Fuck his family," Denny said. "Make sure they are removed from my property and neighborhood by the morning."

Denny looked back at Taina, who was gently touching Chris's cheek. She removed the tape from his mouth as softly as her delicate 9-year-old fingers could, but it still stung.

"Sorry, cousin," she whispered when he jumped slightly.

"Thank you." Chris's voice was barely audible and was drenched with pain. "Thank you so much."

"Papi," Taina told her father, "he needs to go to the hospital. You messed him up pretty good."

Denny walked over to his favorite cousin with regret and sorrow weighing heavily on his heart. He took his cousin's bloody hand, but before he could speak, he felt Chris squeeze.

"N—no apology needed." Chris smiled awkwardly up at Denny through bloody, busted lips "A boss first. J—just get me to the hospital."

"I will make this up to you," Denny promised. "You will have every dime of what you were accused of stealing waiting for you in your bank account as you recover from this."

He wasn't sure if Chris had heard him because he chose that moment to pass out. But it didn't matter because Denny would make good on his word. Denny's men cut Chris free and gently carried him out of the garage. Denny would pay whatever the cost to get Chris back in shape. He should have known that he would never cross him like that. Diablo was closest to Chris when it came to work. He had access to almost as much knowledge of Denny's operations as Chris. Therefore, he must have hacked into some information to steal the money. It must have been going on for years. Denny made a mental note to open up all new accounts and change the combinations to all his locks.

"You almost killed him, Papi!" Taina's voice interrupted Denny's thoughts. "You almost killed Chris."

Denny gripped Taina's shoulders and knelt so they were at eye level. He sighed.

"My child, I never wanted you to see any of this, but since you have, I want to be all the way honest with you. This may not be the last time you see such an act. You will understand one day, just as Chris understands what happened here. Sometimes, you have to cut off your fingers to save your hand for the greater good of the business. But I will forever be thankful that you intervened tonight. I love you, princess."

His words that night would stay with her forever. She blinked back the tears and allowed her father to kiss her forehead. Denny stood up, grabbing his only child's tiny hand, and the two exited the now-empty garage and headed back into the warmth of their home. Taina looked back at the chair that Chris was once strapped to. Her gaze lingered on all the blood surrounding it, knowing that it was an image that she might need to get used to seeing.

# Chapter 2

As Taina grew up, she became a very difficult child. She stopped listening to her mother and father's discipline when she turned 13, but didn't let her parents know. She made it seem like their word was law to their faces, but as soon as they were out of eyesight, she became the real her. She was an only child; most days, it was just her and the housekeepers at home. When her father was out handling business in the streets, her mother, Isabella, was trying to find her purpose. Being the wife of a kingpin was not one of the things she had on her bucket list. It was just how things played out. She wasn't even ready to have a child, which was why Taina was her first and only one. No matter how she tried to connect with her, she couldn't.

Taina would try to tell her that going out to dinner when Isabella didn't have plans or watching a movie with her once a month didn't cut it. Her mother thought that putting forth minimal effort was enough. Taina was jealous of the girls in her middle school class who came to school talking about how much fun they had with their parents and the trips they took. Taina, of course, took trips with her parents, but they were constantly interrupted by her father's business calls or the fact that her mother wanted to get away from both of them. The only time she really got to see them was on Sundays when her mother decided to have Sunday dinner. It was all beginning to take a toll on Taina, and the only one who seemed to notice was her personal housekeeper, Stephanie.

Stephanie had been overseeing Taina since she was a baby, and when she noticed the change, she tried to bring it up to Isabella, who was in the kitchen washing dishes, or that was what she called herself doing. Stephanie and the other housekeepers would always have to go back over her cleaning job.

"Ma'am?" Stephanie spoke to Isabella's back.

Hearing Stephanie's voice, Isabella turned around, and when she saw Stephanie's plump frame behind her, she gave a fake smile.

"Hey, Stephanie," Isabella said, drying her hands off on the dishrag that hung by the sink. "Does Taina need anything?"

"Aren't you her mother?" Stephanie asked, causing Isabella to raise her brow.

"*Excuse* me?" she asked Stephanie, daring her to repeat herself.

"I said, aren't you her mother? Shouldn't you know what she needs?"

"Really bold, Stephanie. But yes, I should know what she needs, and that's why you're here to tell me."

Stephanie shook her head and took in the image of the beautiful, five-foot-four woman before her. Her Christian Dior heels gave her a few more inches of height, and the sleek beige pants suit clenched onto her fit body for dear life. Isabella's face was blemish free, and although she was in her midthirties, she didn't look a day over twenty-five. Stephanie could not say that Isabella was not beautiful, but she felt as though that was all her head was wrapped around. The real reason she never had another child was because she didn't want to ruin her figure. She said it took her too long to bounce back after Taina and refused to put her body through that again.

"Well, yes, Taina does need something," Stephanie finally said.

"Well?" Isabella put her hands in the air for emphasis. "What is it?"

"Taina has been acting differently ever since she started the eighth grade. Her teachers keep calling home and saying she's being a distraction in class. There have even been some fights. The only reason she hasn't been suspended or even expelled is because of who her father is."

"OK, Stephanie. She's a kid. That's what kids her age do. They talk, and they fight."

"I understand that, but how she's acting is not okay. It's not normal."

"Well, as you can see, Taina isn't a normal girl her age. Her father is a fucking kingpin, for crying out loud. And that isn't exactly a secret in this house."

"All I'm saying, *ma'am,* is that you and your husband might want to spend some quality time with her while you still can. I think you should form a better relationship with her."

Isabella looked at Stephanie as if she were a fly on the wall.

"Who do you think you are? Coming in here and telling me what *I* should do with *my* child? Are *you* her parent? And if it is so important to you, why don't you just tell her this?"

Stephanie had finally had enough. She looked at Isabella with the same type of contempt in her eyes.

"No, I'm *not* her mother, but I might as well be. I have been her caretaker since she was a baby, and it is true when I say everything you take credit for, *I* taught her. I have watched her grow these last few years of her life, and each day she becomes sadder and sadder. If you paid enough attention, you would see this too."

Isabella tried to speak, but Stephanie held up her hand to shut her up and continued speaking.

"Now, I can talk to that girl until I'm blue in the face, but you see, she didn't come from my womb, so I don't think it has the same effect. She doesn't feel loved. She feels pushed to the side. This is the last year you'll have her before she's gone to you forever. Once high school gets a hold of her, and she has *that* attitude, not even the fact that her father is the deadliest man in this state will be able to put fear in that child's heart."

Stephanie left Isabella standing there looking dumbfounded and went back upstairs to check on a sleeping Taina. Stephanie could only hope that she'd gotten through to Isabella and that maybe she would pass the message on to Denny, but the following weeks showed her that her words had once again fallen on deaf ears. The saying that you could lead a horse to water but can't make it drink was absolutely true. The warning Stephanie had given should have been heeded. She knew how it went; she was the eldest of five children. She had seen it all. She also knew that once a good girl turned bad, she was gone forever, and Taina had already gotten a taste of that life.

For the rest of Taina's eighth-grade year, Stephanie tried her best to keep her in check, but it proved challenging to do when her father showered her with gifts even though she acted a fool in school. There was no positive or negative reinforcement because Taina got everything she wanted and even things she didn't want. Stephanie knew the reason for the gifts was because Denny felt guilty for being so disconnected from his daughter, but everyone knew that Denny's first love was his business. He had left it up to everyone else to raise his child. He didn't understand that although he had an iron grip on the streets and his business, he was leaving his child to grow up with only herself for guidance.

Stephanie knew that things had finally made a turn for the worse the day she caught Taina smoking marijuana in the bathroom of her bedroom. Stephanie was so caught off guard that she didn't know what to do when Taina opened the door. Her eyes were low and bloodshot red.

"Taina?" Stephanie called out to the 13-year-old.

In response, Taina gave her a dopey smile and tried to shut the bathroom door behind her. But it was too late because Stephanie had already smelled the potent aroma and saw the smoke.

"Oh my God," Stephanie said. "You're high as a freaking kite."

"I'm OK, I'm OK." Taina tried to assure her and went to lie on her bed. "I feel so good right now."

"Where did you get it?"

"You know the other caregivers smoke on all their breaks." Taina giggled and snuggled into her pillow. "I just snatched it from one of their bags. It's some good stuff too."

"*Por qué?*" Stephanie asked. "Why do you feel the need to be high? How long have you been smoking?"

She went over to Taina's bed and lay beside her in her work clothes. Taina smelled strongly of the product and smoke, but that didn't stop Stephanie from pulling her close.

"I just need something to balance out my lows," Taina told her, then started laughing like she had just told the world's funniest joke. "And I've been smoking for about five months now. I usually use eyedrops, so you guys can never tell."

"Oh, honey." Stephanie just shook her head. "I feel like I'm losing you."

"You will never lose me, Steph," Taina said while yawning. "But everyone else might as well have already said goodbye. I'm done aiming to please the two people who created me, especially when I'm invisible to them. They don't care about me . . . They only care about themselves. Well, it's time for me to start doing the same thing."

"Oh, honey," was all Stephanie could say.

She could chastise Taina all she wanted, but she knew that there was no point. It was too late, and she knew whatever she said would just go over her pretty brunette head. It hurt Stephanie to know that the reason Taina smoked was to numb the feeling of emptiness that she had been feeling for so long. After that incident, Stephanie tried her best to fill a little bit of that void over the next few years, but what she soon found was that all she was doing was reminding Taina that her parents weren't active in her life.

Denny had noticed how distant his daughter was from him during her first few years of high school. He also noticed how slick her mouth was, and he constantly had to put her in her place. He was upset with Isabella because she was supposed to be the stay-at-home parent and teach their daughter morals and values, but then again, he couldn't be too upset. The only family-oriented thing that she did was make dinner on some Sundays. He knew when he married her that she was too self-centered to be a mother. He knew Isabella loved Taina very much, but she just didn't know how to be a mother. It was easier letting the help do the job they were too busy to do.

The guilt set in once he realized that his only child was almost an adult and he barely knew her. The housekeepers knew everything about her, but he still thought her favorite food was ice cream and cake. He stepped back from his business to form a better relationship with his daughter before it was too late.

"You're just like me, you know that?" he told her one night after they'd gone to see a movie.

"How so?" she asked as they walked to the car, arm in arm.

"You're smart, speak your mind, and don't take shit from anybody. I also don't think you have a scared bone in your body."

His words made her smile because they were true for the most part. And he was right. She'd gotten those traits from him. When they reached his Rolls-Royce, he opened the passenger-side door for her to get in, but she hesitated.

"What is it, Taina?"

"I am scared of something, Papi. I'm scared of losing you."

"That's something you'll never have to worry about," Denny said, cupping her chin and kissing her forehead. "I'll always be here."

The pair continued getting closer, and Taina's behavior improved tremendously. Stephanie never told Denny about the weed and hoped that Taina would be smart enough to hide it from her father. He would kill them all if he knew his daughter was under the influence of anything. It seemed like Taina was well on her way back to herself, and at the beginning of her senior year of high school, Denny made a promise to her. He promised that as long as she remained boy free and stayed a virgin, then once she graduated high school, he would put $1 million in her bank account for her to do whatever she wanted with it. Taina was happy with the proposition and didn't care that her father sent his hired hands to watch her closely at her private school. It never crossed her mind that any boy would ever even approach her. She was Denny Capello's daughter, and that made her intimidating. She felt that the promise would be an easy one to keep . . . until it wasn't.

# Chapter 3

"Noooo," 17-year-old Taina moaned into her pillow. She cursed her alarm. "Shut the fuck up."

She threw her covers over her head, trying to block out the sun, only to have them pulled from her head.

"Oh no, you don't," Taina heard her personal housekeeper say. "You won't be late for another day of school. Your father chewed me out the last time your principal called home."

Taina smacked her lips.

"Please, Stephanie," Taina begged. "Just ten more minutes? I went to sleep late last night."

"Nope," Stephanie said and made Taina sit up. "Whose fault was that, huh? How many times have I told you not to go to sleep late on a school night? I bet you didn't even do your homework, did you? Isn't that science project due today?"

Stephanie continued fussing at Taina as she prepared the young girl's clothes for the day. Taina tuned the short, plump woman out and stretched, yawning big. She stood up, forgetting what was in her lap until it fell to the ground, rolled over, and hit Stephanie's white-laced shoe. Taina bit her lip and raised her eyebrows, hoping that Stephanie wouldn't look down. She got no such luck. When Stephanie saw what had thumped against her foot, her hand flew to the apron covering her chest, and her nose twisted up.

"Taina!"

"Well, now you know why I was up so late." Taina stifled a laugh as she motioned to her vibrator lying by Stephanie's foot.

She shrugged, and Stephanie just shook her head. She spoke, but her tongue got lost somewhere in turning her thoughts into actual words.

"You're having sex, Taina?" Stephanie asked Taina, already knowing what Denny would do if he discovered something like that.

"No," Taina said with an attitude. She rolled her eyes, grabbing the underwear that Stephanie had placed on her queen-size bed. "If I were, I wouldn't have to put that thing on my middle finger at night and rub my own puss—"

"My God, Taina!" Stephanie threw her arms Taina's way, making a face. "Why must you talk like that?"

"I'm just being honest. I haven't gone all the way with a boy yet, but I'm 17. I have womanly needs now. I'm sure you remember what it's like. At least I'm touching myself and not letting anyone else do it."

Taina smirked and went to the bathroom to shower. When she finished, she came back out clean and wearing her undergarments. Her body was fully defined, and her brunette hair hung to the middle of her back. After she applied lotion to her cream-colored skin, she put her long hair into a high ponytail. Once her hair was in place, she put on her school uniform: blue pants, a white-collared blouse, and a gray sweater that hung around her shoulders. The pants fit snugly around her waist, and her hips looked good.

"Ohhh! Sí. My ass looks amazing in these pants." She admired herself in the full-length mirror on her bedroom door.

Stephanie scooted Taina out of the room and told her breakfast was on the table. She said that she needed to be out of the house by 7:00 and that a driver would be waiting outside. Taina hurried down the stairs and made her way to the kitchen. She heard her parents' voices in there, so she stopped to listen.

"You really need to learn how to control your anger, Denny," Isabella told her husband. "Remember what happened with Chris?"

Taina remembered far too well, and she heard her father grunt.

"That is old news, my dear," Denny said. "Chris has long since forgotten about that incident and has retained his position as my most trusted."

"Well, regardless of that, you need to get it intact. It's starting to get out of control."

"My anger is how I keep control," Denny responded, and Taina heard papers shake.

She smiled, knowing her father was reading the newspaper and probably drinking coffee. She imagined her mother smiling at her father's smart mouth like she always did and saying . . .

"You get on my nerves," Isabella said just as Taina thought it.

"I'm a man. That's what we do," Denny said.

Taina walked in on the two of them just as her father grabbed her mother for a playful hug. They were still laughing when they finally noticed their child's presence. Denny sat wearing an all-black Versace suit that accented his muscular frame. His brown hair had a few gray streaks, but that didn't detract from his youthful face. Many women sent lustful eyes Denny's way, but he let everyone know that he only had eyes for one woman, and that was his wife. Denny checked the gold Rolex on his wrist and gave a faux gasp.

"Who are you, and what have you done with my daughter?" Denny said, letting go of Isabella and picking up his newspaper again.

Taina giggled and took her seat at the kitchen table. Although they had a dining room, her mother kept everyone out of it. Only on Sundays during Sunday dinner were people allowed to enter her sacred room. The kitchen area was spacious. Isabella had a vision for the whole house that she carried out effortlessly. All the appliances were stainless steel, and the cabinet doors were a deep mahogany. The color scheme included many bright colors because Isabella believed that subconsciously, bright colors made you happy. And since most people started their days in the kitchen, then they were bound to have a good day.

"I'm the same me, Papi," Taina said, staring down at the plate already made before her. "You can thank Stephanie. She forced me to get up."

"Good," Denny said. "I've been thinking it feels like I rarely see you anymore. How about I take you shopping before I head to California this weekend?"

Taina used her fork to scoot her bacon around the french toast on her plate. She knew her father would want a response, but she couldn't give him the one he wanted.

"Papi, what's the point in shopping when nobody will even see me in any of the beautiful things you buy me?" she said dully. "I still have tons of bags with clothes and jewelry that I haven't even worn yet."

Denny sighed deeply, knowing that she was right. Growing up the only child of a drug kingpin couldn't have been easy, and Denny sympathized with her for that. It probably didn't make it any easier that he kept a tight hold on her, making it hard for Taina to create her own identity. School was the only getaway that she got, but even that wasn't enough.

Taina was convinced that her parents just didn't understand her. Her thought process differed from theirs, and it annoyed her that they acted as if she didn't know what was happening around her. She had seen firsthand what kind of man her father was at an early age. She knew what he was capable of. Every time Denny got free time, he thought that taking Taina shopping would make up for all the important events in her life that he had missed. But Taina felt obliged to let him know that he couldn't buy her love. She also was annoyed that after all the time they'd spent together, she thought he'd learned by now that material things meant nothing to her. She wanted to see the world and do fun things like scuba diving and base jumping. To him, he thought they had a good relationship, but to Taina, they couldn't have been on further ends of the totem pole.

Taina looked to Isabella, who, instead of backing her up, placed her hand on Denny's shoulder and threw daggers with her eyes at her daughter.

"Don't take that tone with your father, young lady. He works hard, and all he's saying is that he wants to spend some time with you."

"I was just—"

"Just what? Being ungrateful? Most girls with fathers like yours don't even get to see them because they're too busy."

"Fathers like what?" Taina shot back, irritated that her mother had used that moment to attack her. "Oh, you mean drug dealers? Murderers? And wow, finally, you speak. You're like seventeen years too late, though."

Isabella's hand flew to her chest like Stephanie's, and her mouth kept opening and closing while she tried to find the words to say. On the other hand, Denny had placed his chin on his clasped knuckles. He peered into his daughter's eyes and was almost surprised to see that they were empty . . . They reflected his perfectly. It alarmed him. He opened his mouth to say something, but

Taina rolled her eyes hard and pushed away from the table.

"Sit down," Isabella said, but Taina didn't listen and continued to put on her coat.

"Sit down!"

That time, the command came from Denny, and Taina heard the venom in his tone. She knew she best not try her luck with her father, so she dropped back down into the seat with a sigh.

"You will listen to your mother," he said.

"You mean Stephanie?" Taina glared at her mother. "She's upstairs."

Tears came to Isabella's eyes at her daughter's low blow.

Denny looked as if he couldn't believe what he was hearing, but he only had himself to blame. He thought they had formed a good relationship, but it hit him then that a lot of work still needed to be done. He wanted to say so much to his daughter, but unfortunately, he didn't have time. What he didn't understand was that was the exact reason resentment was growing in his daughter's heart.

"I don't have time for this right now," Denny told Taina. "While I'm gone, you will obey everything your mother says. Is that understood?"

"Yes," Taina said through gritted teeth.

"Good," Denny said, smirking at her discomfort. "Now you are dismissed. There is a car waiting to take you to school. And roll those eyes of yours again, and I'll show you one of the many ways I can gouge them out."

Taina took her leave, making sure to keep her eyes in place, and exited the house. She looked around her neighborhood; every house her eyes saw was her father's. Before she was even born, Denny had bought a large piece of land. He had houses built from the ground up for his family and most trusted on that land. Around his land was a gate with a secured entrance, so in a way, he had created his own little community. What was better than being surrounded by people he loved *and* trusted?

The sun was shining, and Taina walked toward the black Audi Q5 hybrid waiting to drive her to school. Before she got to the car, her driver, Thomas, was already holding her door open for her to get in.

"Hello, princess," Thomas said, smiling at Taina. "You look delightful this morning."

Taina muttered something rude under her breath, grabbing her door and slamming it shut. She rolled the middle console up so that she wouldn't be forced into having a conversation. The day had just started, and she was already completely over it.

# Chapter 4

The moment Thomas pulled up in front of Taina's school, she pulled her hair out of the ponytail it was in and applied red lipstick to her lips. She shut the door behind her and quickly became a part of the large swarm of students all making their way up a set of stairs to the tall metal double doors of the school. Whipping her hair over her shoulder with her hand, she looked to the right and saw one of her father's hired hands standing off the stairs watching her to make sure she entered the school safely. She looked to her left and saw the same thing. She groaned and put her head down, running up the remainder of the steps. Being the daughter of Denny Capello had its perks, but it also made it extremely difficult to live the life of an ordinary teenage girl.

During the previous three years of schooling, Denny made one of his men shadow her to every class, while another sat outside the classroom daily. It was something the other kids talked badly about behind her back. Everyone thought she felt as if she were better than them, and that wasn't the case at all. If only they knew how jealous she was of their everyday lives. That year, her senior year, Taina talked her father into laying off a little bit. Instead of having someone walk her to class every day like a baby, they could just patrol the whole school while she was there. She told him she was almost a grown woman and needed to find her own sense of independence. Also, it was hard to do that when everywhere she looked, she was reminded of who her father was, and so was everyone else. Taina had never made any real friends because everyone was skeptical of getting too close to her.

She refused to graduate high school without getting any of its classic effects, so she vowed that her senior year would be different, and so far, it had been. She had a group of friends that she clicked with and was having a good year. Her grades were very important since it was the middle of the school year, or so her mother said. But Taina knew, just like her mother, that she wouldn't have to work a day in her life if she didn't want to. She was sure that she was only in school because the law required her to be there. Taina wasn't a bad kid, but since school was the only time she got a little bit of freedom, she took advantage of it. She often skipped class to hang out with her friends and do other things she had no business doing.

Taina walked into her first class, English, and shined her perfect teeth at her close friend, Marisol, who she spotted right away in the back of the classroom. Marisol was sitting beside an empty desk, and Taina knew she was saving it for her. Marisol was a petite, pretty girl. She had fire-red hair cut into a bob that was longer on the right side of her face. Her emerald-green eyes set the mood in any room she entered, and her high cheekbones demanded the attention of everyone within a looking distance. Although she wasn't shapely like Taina, she had her own look going for her.

Taina started to make her way to the back of the classroom when a whisper stopped her. She looked to her right and saw one of the girls, Selena Ramos, who had hated her since she started attending school there. She lived right outside Denny's gated community with her family and always thought Taina had an uppity attitude. Taina blew her a kiss and kept walking.

"What's up, bitch?" Taina greeted Marisol and plopped down in the seat next to her.

"Hey, girl. Why didn't you call me back last night?" Marisol inquired.

Taina thought back to the events of the night before and smirked. "I had some business to handle," she said with a sly smile, and Marisol burst out laughing.

"Oh my God, girl," Marisol said, wiping the tears from her eyes. "You are nasty. You need to get some dick and stop playing with yourself. Literally."

Taina laughed too.

"It's not exactly that easy. You know who my father is." Taina gave Marisol a knowing look. "He would kill me and whatever ingrate stuck his little penis in me."

"Taina!" Marisol laughed again. That time, it made the teacher look their way.

"Are you ladies done talking so can I begin my lesson? Unless one of you wants to come up here and teach the class instead?"

"Sorry, Mrs. Ross," Marisol said. "You can continue."

Mrs. Ross's eyes remained on Taina, and she continued to glare at her. Already knowing where her teacher's dislike for her stemmed from, Taina jerked her neck in disrespect and rolled her eyes.

"Is there a problem, Mrs. Ross?" Taina asked. "Em already said we were done talking. You can teach now."

Mrs. Ross curled her lip, and suddenly, the whole class got quiet. She walked to the back of the class until she was directly in front of Taina.

"Listen here, young lady," she said to the young girl, "I don't care who your father is outside of this classroom, but while you are here, you won't receive any special treatment. Do you understand me?"

Taina looked at Mrs. Ross like she was a joke.

"Do you understand?" Mrs. Ross raised her voice.

"Am I supposed to say, 'Yes, ma'am'?" Taina snapped back. "Because if that's the response you're hoping for, you're sadly mistaken. You *may* teach the class, though."

"Get out of my classroom now," Mrs. Ross yelled and pointed at the door, offended by Taina's audacity.

"Again?" Marisol said. "She didn't even do nothing."

"It's cool, Em," Taina, who hadn't even gotten settled in her seat, stood up and said. "I know what this is really about." She threw her book bag over her shoulder and got in Mrs. Ross's face. "This bitch has had it out for me since the first day of school. What? Are you still mad that my father fucked you and then stopped returning your calls?"

Mrs. Ross gasped and looked at Taina like she wanted to smack the smug look from her pretty little face.

"Damn," Taina taunted. "I hit a nerve, huh? My mother told me all about you. Why do you think that whenever you get the principal to call home about me, she doesn't do shit about it? Because she knows that you are just a bitter-ass woman who married a man you didn't love because the man you *wanted* married someone else. Get out of my way."

Taina left Mrs. Ross standing there stunned and moved past her. On her way out of the classroom, Selena stuck her foot out in the aisle to be funny. Taina saw it just in time and shot Selena a mean look.

"Bitch, don't get fucked up," Selena sneered at her rival. "Your father isn't here to protect you now."

Taina finally had had enough of Selena's smart mouth. She slapped her so hard that a red hand imprint immediately formed on her cheek. But Taina didn't stop there. She threw her book bag off her back and commenced beating Selena's face. The whole class had gathered around the two girls, and Mrs. Ross scrambled to call security. A few of Selena's friends saw her getting the life beat out of her and tried to intervene. One grabbed

Taina's hair while the other tried to get in a few hits. Marisol wasn't having any of that.

"Uh-uh. You whores aren't about to jump my bitch," she yelled and got the girls off Taina.

It wasn't the first fight Taina and Marisol had gotten into together, but they always shut things down. The two girls came out with a few scrapes and bruises, but they always looked better than their opponents. That time was no different.

"Come on, let's go before those fuck boys show up," Taina said and grabbed her book bag off the floor and Marisol's hand so that they could run out of the classroom together.

When they were out in the hallway, they decided to go to the usual spot where they cut class together, behind the stairwell at the very back of the school.

"Fuck," Marisol said when they sat on the cold marble floor. "We were just about to get to my favorite part in *Hamlet.*"

"You are *such* a nerd, dude," Taina said, unzipping her bag. "Where the trees at?"

She took out a pack of regular Swisher Sweets cigarillos and removed one from the pack. Then she gutted it, and Marisol took out her weed and broke it down with her pink grinder.

"This is some good shit," Marisol said. "I got it from my brother's stash."

"One day, he's going to find out you've been stealing his weed." Taina giggled.

"Well, for your sake, you better hope he doesn't. Here." She handed the broken down weed to Taina, who put it in the brown wrap.

She rolled the blunt so perfectly that a pothead would have envied it. The two girls took turns hitting the blunt and passing it.

"I'm glad you finally beat Selena's ass," Marisol said. "Everybody thinks you're some frail princess, but you showed them fuckers today."

Taina nodded her head. Her father taught her how to fight when she was very young, despite her mother's dislike.

"I hate that bitch," Taina said. "She's such a hater. Mrs. Ross too. My mom said she tried to trap my papi with a kid and . . . Well, you don't want to know what my mom did. Anyways, what did you say this shit was called again? 'Cause it's hitting."

"I didn't say," a high Marisol laughed. "But my brother said it's called Starburst or something. I told you it was some good shit."

When they finished smoking, their eyes were low and bloodshot red. Knowing that they had more classes to go to, Marisol took out some eyedrops for them to use and some perfume spray.

"That's why you're my bitch," Taina said as she used the drops.

Just as they finished getting rid of the evidence and took one step from behind the stairwell, they saw one of the school security guards and the principal headed their way. Marisol hurriedly stuffed the grinder in her book bag, and the girls walked toward the two men.

"What's up, Principal Schroeder?" Marisol asked, her voice low and even.

Principal Schroeder was a man in his late forties with a head full of white hair. His face held many wrinkles from frowning at the students who frequented his office daily. That day he'd heard an urgent request for security being called for Taina Capello over his walkie-talkie. From the sounds of it, he knew he'd better be present for the pickup, but upon arriving at the classroom, he was informed that she and Marisol Ramos had fled. He searched the empty halls of the school for the two girls for more than thirty minutes before he finally found them.

"Hey, Principal Schroeder," Taina greeted him in a stoner trance.

He looked back and forth between the two young women and noticed something was off about them. He knew they were high out of their minds by the grins on their faces and the fact that the tops of their eyelids were basically touching their bottom ones. He breathed deeply and looked at the security officer standing slightly behind him.

"Take Marisol and escort her to her next class," he said. "Taina, you come with me."

The girls went to protest, but one stern look from Principal Schroeder silenced them.

"See you at lunch, *chica*," Marisol said to Taina before the young security guard led her off.

"Follow me," Principal Schroeder instructed Taina.

She followed him, already knowing he was about to take her to his office to talk with her one-on-one. It never failed. He saw Taina in his office every other week or once a month. Either way, it was far too much for his liking. He led her through the whole school until they got to his office, where he opened the doors and walked through with Taina close behind him. She smiled at the young secretaries, who shook their heads when they saw her.

"Not again, Taina," one of them named Jen said.

She was the only one Taina seemed to like in the whole office. She stared at Taina with knowing eyes. Instead of responding with words, Taina put her hands up and shrugged her shoulders. She was sure that Jen knew all about the fight.

Taina followed Principal Schroeder back. He opened a glass door leading to his office. The office was spacious and neat. The walls were off-white, and he had a flat-screen TV hanging from the ceiling. She looked around at all his pictures on the walls.

*That's when he went fishing. That's when his wife had their son. That's when he became principal.*

Taina mentally recited the happenings of his photos as she sat down across Principal Schroeder's desk. He stared into her eyes briefly as if waiting for her to speak first. When she didn't say a word, he sighed. Taina's folder was already sitting on his desk, but he pushed it aside instead of looking through it.

"Aren't you growing tired of seeing my office?"

"Never," she said with a smile. "It's so interesting here. Why would I ever get tired of seeing such a place?"

The principal heard the sarcasm in her voice and shook his head.

"I think you behaved much better when your father had those bodyguards accompanying you to class," he said.

"I would be just fine if you would tell the teachers here to watch their mouths," Taina snapped back. "I would never get in trouble if people just talked to me right."

"You are a student. It is your responsibility to respect the teachers. And fighting is something we can't tolerate in this school."

"So, basically, you're saying that it is OK for these teachers to talk to me crazy, but I can't defend myself verbally? And it is OK for a girl to try to trip me just as long as I don't hit her back? Why isn't *she* in the office too?"

"She is in the nurse's office, that's why."

"That's what that bitch gets," Taina said, folding her arms with a smug expression. She leaned back in her seat and looked the principal square in his eyes. "Because I'm sure that's the only form of discipline she will receive."

"Look, Taina, I'm not sure what happened in that classroom today. All I know is that several witnesses are saying that you took your frustration with Mrs. Ross out on Selena."

"And how believable does that sound, Schroeder? Whenever I come into your stupid office, you never believe me or anything I say. So you know what? Forget it. Give me detention, in-school suspension, or whatever. I don't care."

Principal Schroeder thumbed through her file and saw it read of a troubled kid. No discipline seemed to work with her, and whenever he called home, one of the Capellos' many housekeepers always answered the phone. He had tried to schedule conferences with her parents, but only her mother always came. And he felt that Taina and her mother didn't exactly see eye to eye when it came to certain things.

"It's to the point where I don't know what to do with you anymore, Taina. And because your father made one of the most generous donations to the school, I am not able to suspend or expel you."

Taina translated that to, "Your father put too much money into this school that we have already spent, so I know that if I get rid of you, Denny Capello will kill me."

She shook her head. Nobody cared about her, and Principal Schroeder's following statement proved that.

"Just do me a favor and *try* to keep your nose clean for the next few months, OK? You get good enough grades, and you graduate soon. The sooner you can get your diploma, the sooner you can be out of this school and out of my hair. Deal?"

"Whatever," she responded, looking at the ground.

Suddenly, there was a knock on the door of his office. Before he could answer, the secretary Jen opened it.

"I'm sorry to interrupt, sir, but I have a student here looking for his class schedule. He's the new student."

"No problem, I was just done here," Principal Schroeder said. "Send him on in."

Taina glanced up when she heard footsteps walking inside the office. Her heart skipped a beat when they fell on the most handsome boy she had ever seen in her life. He was a tall Latino and had the most gorgeous eyes in the universe. His brown hair was a nice length, not too long or too short, but trimmed nicely.

When he saw Taina staring, he flashed her a perfect white smile, and his already high cheekbones rose even higher. He was a pretty boy, but something about him read the complete opposite of that. He was dressed in the school uniform, but Taina was drooling at the sight of his muscles that were defined clear as day through his blazer.

"Hey," he said to her.

"H . . . hey." Taina swallowed her spit and waved a shaky hand.

"Jen, can you please get somebody to escort Taina back to class for me? I'm not sending her home today, but I also don't want any more fights breaking out in the hallways."

Jen winked at Taina, seeing how she looked at the new student.

"Come on, Laila Ali," she said. "Let's get you back to class."

Taina stood up, and the boy took her seat. She was about to follow Jen, but right before she exited the office, she heard the boy's voice being directed at her again.

"Taina," he said, causing her to whip her head around. "I like that name."

"Thank you." She returned his smile. "What's your name?"

"Mario."

"Mario? Hmm . . . Fits you. Well, I'll see you around, *Mario*."

"I hope so."

Taina hurried up and turned around before he could see her face turn beet red. Jen gave her a knowing look when she shut Principal Schroeder's door behind them. She called a security guard with her walkie-talkie to show Taina to her next class. He showed up in no time, but Jen grabbed her hand gently before he left with Taina.

"Can this please be the last time I see you in this office?" she asked.

"I can't make any promises," Taina told her with a sly smile. "But I can try to make my next visit not so soon."

# Chapter 5

"Oh my gosh, girl, he was so fine," Taina told Marisol at lunch. "I have *never* seen anybody look so good except for, like, on the internet."

Taina had been waiting for her lunch period for what seemed like a whole year. When the bell finally rang in her AP Psychology class, she jetted out of the hallway to meet Marisol in the cafeteria. She spotted Em instantly at the table they sat at every day with a few other girls, but Taina didn't care for them to know her business all like that. She sat down and spoke to her friend in a low, excited voice.

"So is he, like, here for the whole day? Like, did he start school here already?" Marisol asked, happy that her friend finally had a crush.

She had secretly started to think that her friend was going the other way because she never gave any guys at their school a chance. She was genuinely excited to see her girl interested in a boy. She could see the giddiness in Taina's eyes when she spoke about him and could only imagine what he looked like.

"Well, he was getting his class schedule, so I would assume that he did start today. He was also in his uniform."

"See? It was meant for you to beat the shit out of Selena today. If you hadn't done that, you wouldn't have had to go to the office, and you wouldn't have met the man of your dreams."

Taina burst out laughing. Marisol was really into that "destiny" mumbo jumbo, and she truly felt that everything happened for a reason, that there was never anything left up to chance.

"Uh, man of my dreams?" Taina raised her eyebrow, still laughing. "I don't know about that, but he is sexy. Come on. There are enough girls here to hold the table down. Let's get in the lunch line."

The two of them walked through all the students who had lunch that period to get to one of the two lunch lines in the middle of the cafeteria. They pouted because the line was so long, and they had to take their place behind it.

"Taina?"

Taina heard a familiar voice call her name. She leaned back and looked up the line. What she saw made her smile. Mario was waving at her and telling the two of them to come cut him in line.

"Come on." Taina grabbed Marisol's hand and dragged her to the front of the line.

When Marisol's eyes laid on Mario, she understood why her friend's mind was so gone. The boy was fine.

"Well, uh, hello," Marisol said, nudging Taina with her shoulder, giving her the silent "OK."

"Hey." Mario flashed them a charming smile. "You are?"

"Her best friend. My name is Marisol. I already know your name. No need to introduce yourself."

If looks could kill, Taina would have sent Marisol to an early death. Mario saw this and burst out laughing.

"Well, I'm glad I could make a lasting impression." He winked at a very embarrassed and speechless Taina.

Luckily for her, it was her turn to grab a tray and choose her lunch. Taina wasn't a salad-eating girl, so she chose a greasy hamburger and fries and bought a lemonade with the tab her father had for her. When she reached the end of the line, she entered in her school ID and waited for the other two to join her.

"Do you have anywhere to sit?" Taina asked Mario. "If not, you can sit with us."

She looked at the table they had just come from and saw only two available seats. She looked at Marisol for help, knowing that this might be her only chance to make an impression on him. She'd already seen the other girls eyeing him like a hawk, and she wanted to sink her claws in him first. Marisol was quick on her feet. She spotted an empty table not too far from where they were standing and pointed it out to them.

"You two go sit over there," Marisol said. "I'll go sit at our usual table. I'll see you after school, B."

She gave Mario another look of approval before taking her food tray back to the table she originated from. Taina led the way to the table Marisol pointed out, noticing all the jealous looks thrown her way. She spotted Selena at a table with all her friends staring hatefully at her as she sat alone with Mario.

"So," Taina started when they were across from each other, "what's up with you? Why did you transfer here when the school year is almost up? Are you a senior?"

Mario looked at Taina with a blank face. "I mean, can I start my food before you start asking me all these questions?"

Taina instantly knew that she had messed up.

"I . . . I'm sor—" She stopped in the middle of her apology when Mario burst into a grin.

"Hey, I'm just fuckin' with you. Chill."

"You dick." Taina swatted him playfully on the arm.

"Nah, seriously, I'm not about to eat this nasty shit anyways," he said, making a face at his plate. "This shit looks deadly."

Taina laughed so hard she almost choked on the piece of burger in her mouth.

"See? I'm cool on that."

"You're so stupid," Taina said, still laughing.

"Never that." Mario winked at her, causing her to blush. "But to answer your questions, my family moves a lot. Well, what I have left of a family. When my uncle died, it kind of tore up my family. Nobody has gotten along in years. I moved here with a different uncle and aunt not too long ago. She gave me a choice of working or finishing my senior year."

"That's deep," Taina said, adding shyly, "Well, I'm glad they chose New York as the move."

"Me too . . . now." Mario grabbed Taina's hand, using his thumb to rub it.

*OK . . . Is this what happens in the movies? Does it happen this fast? OK, Taina . . . breathe. Don't trip out and scare him away,* she thought, trying to force the butterflies out of her stomach.

"Now, what about you? So far, all I know is that you're the most beautiful girl in the school, and you like to fight. I'm sure there is more to your storybook."

"Well, if you must know, yes, I did fight today . . . I've gotten into a lot of fights, actually," she said, using her free hand to play with the food on her tray. "But the truth is that I hate to fight. I don't like causing other people physical pain. You have to really push me to that point. And at this school, I get tested a lot because of who my father is."

"What? Does he own the school or something?"

"No, but he runs the streets of New York." Taina sighed.

"You say that like your dad is Denny Capello or something." Mario laughed and looked at Taina, hoping she would laugh with him.

When she didn't, he quickly pulled his hand away from hers like he was touching some off-limits property.

"See," Taina said to him, shaking her head. "Now you're going to treat me like I'm poisonous just like everyone else."

Mario saw that he had genuinely hurt Taina's feelings and replaced his hand on top of hers. But as he did so, he looked around, and Taina seemed to know exactly what he was looking for.

"My father decided to give me a little more space this year—no more goons following me around. I got tired of being crowded all the time. I just want to be a normal girl."

"Well, I'm sorry to put it to you like this, but you're something like a princess . . . There ain't nothing normal about that."

Taina made a face at him.

"Thanks. Thanks a lot."

"I'm just saying, but why would he not have anybody here to protect you?"

"Oh, trust me, they're here. They're outside of the building, though, making sure that everybody who isn't supposed to be here stays out while I'm in here."

"Smart," Mario said.

"He better be smart since all he seems to have time for is work these days," Taina said with a little bit of salt in her voice.

"You aren't very close, I'm guessing."

"Nope."

"Well, don't take it to heart. I don't know what his life is like, but I can only assume it's very hectic."

"Fuck that. He shouldn't have had a kid then."

"Ooookay," Mario said, realizing his words hadn't really helped any.

"I'm sorry." Taina knew she was targeting her bitterness at the wrong person. "I didn't mean to sound like a bitch."

At that moment, the bell rang, signaling that their lunch period was now over. Mario grabbed both of their trays and took them to the trash can.

*Great. You just blew your chance with him,* Taina thought, standing to her feet.

Mario came back to the table and grabbed his book bag.

"I have a way you can make it up to me," he said, interrupting her negative thoughts. "Go out with me this weekend? To dinner on Saturday . . . We can go to a movie too, but I don't really do movies like that."

"That's perfect," Taina said a little too fast. "I mean, uhh, let me check my schedule, and I'll get back to you. Here, take my number."

She hurried up and gave him her number. Looking over his shoulder, she saw Marisol standing at one of the cafeteria exits, looking impatient. She grinned, knowing that Marisol was dying to know what had transpired during their lunch period. She told Mario she would see him later and walked away without looking back. When she reached Marisol, the two girls linked arms and bustled their way through the cluster of students in the hallway.

"Soooo?" Marisol shook her arm a little bit. "You're killing me."

"I like him," Taina said with a dreamy look. "I like him a lot."


Taina went to Marisol's house that day after school to review their earlier homework. She texted her mother when her driver drove her and Marisol away from the school. When they arrived at Marisol's house, Taina said a quick hello to her mother and kissed Marisol's little brother, Eduardo, on his forehead. Marisol led the way to her bedroom, and once there, both girls threw their book bags to the side.

"Well, I guess they haven't called home yet," Marisol said. "My mom is being nice."

"They probably already called my house," Taina said. "I doubt Stephanie told my mom, though. You know she doesn't give a fuck about what I do. There would be no point."

"That's crazy," Marisol said. "Anyways, back to *Marioooo*."

The singsong voice she used made Taina roll her eyes.

"What about him?" Taina tried to sound nonchalant.

"Bitch, now it's 'what about him,' when you were just hella geeked at the school behind his ass."

"Nah, I'm just kidding," Taina said, grinning. "He's just so cool. I don't know, but there is just something about him that I like. He's not like the other guys at school, from what I can tell anyway. He didn't even care that I was Denny Capello's daughter. I was just Taina at the lunch table today, and you don't know how good that felt, Marisol."

"Well, shit." Marisol winked. "You're always just Taina to me. You don't get special treatment, chica."

"Shut up," Taina said, smiling dreamily. "I'm trying to be serious with you."

At that moment, she felt her smartphone vibrate in her pocket. When she checked the name, she squealed excitedly and used her butt to bounce up and down on Marisol's bed.

"It's him!"

"What'd he say?"

"Ummm." Tiana checked the message. "He said, 'Wassup ma?' Ahhh . . . What should I say? What should I say? I don't want to sound too geeked. Should I wait like ten minutes before texting back?"

Marisol looked at Taina like she was an alien and burst out laughing.

"Marisol." Taina poked her lip out and looked desperately at her friend for help.

She had never really talked to a boy she liked so much and didn't want to mess it up by saying the wrong thing.

"Okay, okay, okay," Marisol said. "Just ask him about how his day was. That's always a good conversation starter, and then after that, just let it flow naturally, chica."

"OK," Taina said, sending the text, and while she sent it, Marisol was eyeing her.

"Girl, before you get that pretty head wrapped up in a boy, just remember the rules of the game."

Taina raised an eyebrow and cocked her head to the side. "Rules? What rules?"

"Rule number one is never to give too much too soon. Rule number two is never to lose yourself behind any guy. And rule three is always to remember you are beautiful and young. The guy you meet now most likely isn't who you'll marry, so there isn't really a point in trying to get in too deep."

"You mean fall in love?"

"Exactly."

"OK, Confucius," Taina said sarcastically.

"I'm being serious, B." Marisol laughed. "For real, just follow those rules, and I promise you will be saved from a world of heartbreak."

"Well, I firmly believe in following whatever path you're on at the moment."

"Bitch, you just made that shit up."

"So?" Taina laughed.

Taina stayed over at Marisol's house for the next few hours. She texted Mario on and off, and the girls finished their homework. She knew that having her homework done by the time she got home would save her from receiving a bad verbal lashing from Stephanie. Taina pictured Stephanie sitting on her bed, waiting for her to walk through the bedroom door, just *ready* to dig in.

When it was time for them to say goodbye, the two girls hugged each other tightly like they would never see each other again.

"See you at school." Marisol waved to Taina before her driver took off.

Taina waved back out of the window, then rolled it up. She had just gotten comfortable in her seat when her phone vibrated again. She grinned when she read the message on her screen.

There's just something about you. I don't know what it is, but I can't get you out of my mind. Call me when you get home?

Taina quickly sent him an "OK" text and held the phone to her chest with her eyes closed. She silently willed Thomas to drive faster so she could hurry up and call him. She couldn't wait to hear his voice. She tried to think of different topics to talk about the whole ride so that they wouldn't just be sitting on the phone listening to each other breathing.

Taina barely paid attention to the scenery that the car passed by on the way, but when they finally pulled up, she had never been so grateful to see the gates of their home. That had felt like the longest car ride she'd ever been on.

"Thank you!" Taina said to Thomas, and she hopped out of the vehicle before it was in park.

Thomas sputtered something about her safety, but she didn't hear him. She'd already slammed the door shut. Taina ran into the house and up the stairs toward her bedroom. She looked over the stair railing back to the first floor and saw her mother watching one of her sitcoms in the living room. She didn't even acknowledge the fact that Taina was home. But Taina didn't care. She only had one thing on her mind.

When she reached her room, she took her phone out, preparing to dial Mario's number . . . but a throat being cleared interrupted her in midbutton press. She looked over and saw Stephanie sitting on her bed, checking out the manicure on her short, stubby fingers.

"So, what's this I hear about a fight you had at school?"

"Fuck," Taina said under her breath, already knowing that she was in for a lecture that she would never forget.

# Chapter 6

Denny Capello sat in the plush white seat of his private jet as it made its way to California. He had some major business to wrap up there, but his mind was on everything but business for some reason. He thought about his conversation with his wife right before he left. His words had been harsh, and even though he wished he could take them back, he knew they needed to be said. After Taina's outburst, Isabella sat down at the table with tears falling from her eyes. She looked at Denny and shook her head.

*"I can't believe she said that."*

*"Why not?" Denny said. "She's completely right."*

*Isabella was even more surprised to hear those words from her own husband. She choked on her spit when she tried to catch her sob from coming out.*

*"How can you agree with her? I have done my best to raise that girl."*

*"No, you haven't. Neither one of us has." Denny was looking at his paper, but his eyes didn't focus on any of the words. "We tried . . . but not hard enough. We aren't consistent whenever we try to mend the relationship with her. We give her so much and then take it away from her in a heartbeat."*

*Isabella silently listened to her husband, but she still did not agree with his words. When he paused, she wiped her tears away and spoke again.*

*"I just feel that she has everything she has ever wanted and is ungrateful. I'm tired. I'm tired of getting calls*

*from that school of hers. I'm tired of going up there and meeting with the principal."*

"What I don't understand, my love,"—Denny disregarded everything Isabella had just said—"is that you have been a stay-at-home mom and wife for almost eighteen years. Why isn't your relationship with her better? I'm not making any excuses for myself, but you focus more on yourself than your own child. I do what I must to keep money in our accounts and ensure we will never need anything. What do you do?

"I knew when I married you that you were not the type to take any part in my business ventures, and that is fine. You can keep your hands clean. But I did not know that even after you had a child, you would continue to put yourself first. Why is it that the help know our child more than you do when you should be with her as much as them? I'm not saying it is OK for Taina to speak to you out of turn, and I will handle that, but do you really blame her for feeling the way she does?"

At that moment, Denny's phone rang. He was informed that his car was ready to drive him to his jet when he answered it.

"I have to go," Denny said to his wife. "While I'm gone, think about what I have just said to you. I love you." He kissed her on her forehead and left.

He replayed his words repeatedly as the plane soared through the sky. Out of everything to not have under control, nobody would have guessed that this would be it. He knew he would need to get it in check, or he feared losing his daughter forever.

"Denny."

Denny snapped out of his thoughts and turned his attention toward Chris, who had accompanied him.

"That's the third time I called your name."

"I'm sorry," Denny said, motioning for his flight attendant to pour him a shot of tequila. "I was in deep thought."

"Yeah, I could tell. I knew something was really bothering you. Anything you want to talk about?"

"Nah," Denny said and threw the shot back. "It's just Taina."

"Boys?"

"Hell no. I'll shoot any motherfucker she brings through the door."

"Believe me," Chris said, "I know. But she's almost 18. It's about that time."

"Thank you for your honesty and support," Denny said sarcastically.

Chris was trying to make light of the situation, but he understood. He had been around Taina a few times and noticed how different she was from the child he had once known. She had grown up and become her own person. With a father as busy as Denny, the mother's job was to keep the child well-rounded. That was his take on it, anyway. Chris had warned Denny about marrying a woman like Isabella. She was selfish and didn't know how to connect to a child.

"She's just a teenager who needs some guidance, that's all. If this deal goes without a hitch, you can take a whole year off to dedicate to being a father."

"Not if she goes to college," Denny said sadly.

"College?" Chris scoffed. "What does she need a degree for when she can be a CEO at age 18? We're Capellos. We make our own way. Fuck a degree."

Denny laughed and shook his finger at his cousin.

"You're a crazy fool, man," he said. "I want her to have an education. Who knows, she might go into something in the legal field. If that's the case, I will be firing Bernard."

He spoke of his lawyer, and Chris laughed.

"Just don't stress yourself too much," Chris said. "But times like this, I'm glad my daughter is only 5 years old."

Denny smiled at the mention of his beautiful little cousin, Mia. Just like Taina was the spitting image of him, Mia was the spitting image of her father. Suddenly, regret filled Denny's gut as he remembered that Mia's existence had almost never occurred. If he had killed Chris that night long ago, he would have never had the joy of becoming a father.

"Do you truly forgive me for that night?" Denny asked Chris, looking into his eyes.

"You ask me this question at least twice a year." Chris leaned forward in his seat across from Denny. "Sí, I do. All my bones healed, and I am alive, living well. If the roles had been reversed, I would have done the same thing." He extended his hand. "By shaking my hand now, you promise never to bring that shit up again. My knee gets this weird feeling whenever you make me think back to that day. You have a mean swing. Always have since we were kids."

After the two men shook hands, the pilot announced they were arriving and asjed the to put their seat belts back on to prepare for the landing.

"If you close this deal, Denny, you're going to change the heroin game in both New York *and* Florida."

"If I close the deal?" Denny said, fixing his tie. "I don't travel anywhere unless it's a sure thing. The deal has already closed, and I haven't even shown my face yet."

Denny touched his hip to feel the gun there. He pulled it from his waist and checked the clip.

"How many did you send before us?"

"A whole fleet."

"Good," Denny said. "Rodriguez isn't going to know what hit him. I think the contract will be signed within the hour."

"You're a crazy motherfucker, man," Chris said, checking his own gun.

"If you've noticed, all the greats have been crazy motherfuckers," Denny said. "After today, I'll be on that list."

# Chapter 7

The rest of the week, Taina shocked Stephanie. Whenever she went in to wake her up in the morning, not only was Taina already awake, but she was dressed too. Taina took her time in the morning with her wand curls and put on a little makeup, enough to cover any blemishes but not enough to tell she had any on.

She and Mario had been spending a lot of time together. They texted each other throughout the day, and when they got home from school, they talked on the phone all night. She found out they had so much in common, and she loved that he was a deep thinker. He had dreams of one day becoming a famous architect and designing buildings.

When they were at school, they met up between class periods to talk since Taina hadn't yet figured out a way to see him outside of school. She was still working on how she would make it to their date on Saturday. The only way she could think of was to lie and tell her parents that she was going to Marisol's house for the weekend, but knowing her father, he would still send two men with her for safety. She could try to sneak out Marisol's window, but she'd get caught faster than a cheater who forgot to delete their text messages. As Saturday drew nearer, she finally realized that she would just have to tell her parents flat-out that she had a date. There was no getting around it if she wanted to go.

On Friday, after she got ready for school, she took a deep breath before she went downstairs to speak to her parents. Stephanie came and kissed her on the cheek. Taina had already told her of her dilemma, and she said she would be there for moral support.

"*Ay probrecita,*" Stephanie said and gripped Taina's shoulders. "It won't be so bad. Come on, you must go now, or you'll be late for school. You've been making me so proud, by the way. I should have known there was a boy involved."

Taina began the walk of death down the stairs—at least, that was what it felt like. Stephanie gave her a slight push whenever she was about to stop walking. They walked toward Taina's parents' voices in the kitchen.

"My daughter," Denny said, greeting her. "Sit down. Have some breakfast before you leave."

He saw Stephanie behind Taina but didn't say anything about it. When she didn't sit, Denny looked up again.

"I'm not hungry, Papi," Taina said and then looked back at Stephanie, who did a shooing motion with her hands, urging Taina to continue. "I have something I want to ask you."

Isabella stopped eating her oatmeal and tuned in to the conversation. Denny set his paper aside and gave Taina his undivided attention.

"What is on your mind, princess?"

"You see . . . uh . . ." Taina searched for the words. She couldn't believe that she didn't practice *that* part at all. Finally, she just said forget it and spit it out. "There is this boy at school who I like, and he seems to like me just as much. His name is Mario, and he asked me to go on a date with him on Saturday. I told him I would love to go, but I would have to ask you first, Papi. Can I go?"

Denny looked at Taina as if he had never seen her a day in his life before. He was at a loss for words because that was definitely the last thing he had expected her to say. He had done good and lucked out for almost four years, but now, there he was with the inevitable staring him in the face. He should have known something was up by how Taina carried herself lately. He was forced to see her as a beautiful young lady, not his baby girl. Still, he would try to prolong it for as long as possible.

"What about our agreement, Taina?" he said evenly.

"What about it, Papi?" she asked. "It's just dinner. I want to go, Papi. Please?"

Taina couldn't remember the last time she begged anyone for anything, especially her father, and that should have shown him that she really wanted to go.

"I will not allow it," Denny said, then picked up his paper again. "Tell him that I said no."

"What?" Taina asked incredulously. "Why?"

She knew he might say no, but not just flat-out like that. He didn't even have a reason.

"Because I said so," Denny said. "It is something that is not up for debate. That boy isn't looking at you for you. He's looking to get into your pants or to get in good with me—like they always do."

"He's not like that, Papi. Just give him a chance," Taina tried one more time. She then looked at Isabella for help, but she just shook her head. "I don't understand the point of having a kid when you don't let me do anything. Papi, you don't even have a real reason not to let me go, and, Mom, you are just going based on what Papi says because you don't have a mind of your own. You're just trying to control me, and it's not fair to me. If I can't go, I won't have anything to say to you this whole weekend. Don't come knocking on my door!"

Taina ran out of the kitchen to the waiting car that was to take her to school. Stephanie put her hand on her hip and looked at Denny like he had shit on his face. Denny looked at her venomously, daring her to speak out of turn. Stephanie was bold enough to step out of line and talk crazy to Isabella, but she would never have enough guts to do the same to Denny. Instead, she took her leave and went to find some work to do. She wanted to busy herself to keep Taina's hurt voice off her mind all day.


"He said no," Taina told Mario the second she saw him in the hallway. "He didn't even care to hear me out. He just said no."

Mario used his hand to brush against Taina's cheek gently.

"It's OK, beautiful. I will see you this weekend one way or another."

There was something about Mario's voice that always made Taina want to draw nearer, so she did. Mario leaned against a locker, and she leaned on him. She gazed up into his alluring eyes.

"But how?" she asked.

Instead of answering, Mario leaned down and kissed her softly, which they had often been doing lately. Taina slipped her tongue into his mouth, and she felt one of his hands put pressure on the small of her back while the other cupped her chin. She finally broke the kiss because she had to come up for air. She was sure she was about to faint because everything about Mario was so perfect.

"I'm going to sneak out." It was like a lightbulb flashing in her head. "I'm going to sneak out on Saturday night. I will give you my address, and I want you to wait outside the gate for me to come out at midnight, OK?"

Mario looked down at Taina, trying to read her face. At first, he thought she was joking, but seeing the serious-ness in her expression, he knew she wasn't.

"Are you sure that's a good idea? I'm sure all he needs to do is meet me, and he will be open to me dating his daughter."

"You don't know my father. He would rather hang himself on a fishing hook and be thrown to the sharks than see me grow up and have a boyfriend."

"Boyfriend?" Mario smiled slyly down at Taina.

"W-well, you know what I mean," she said.

"Yeah, I do," Mario said and kissed her again. "It means we are officially together now. Nobody can stop this, not even your father."

The bell that signaled them being almost tardy sounded, and all the students surrounding them began to put a pep in their steps.

"I better get going too," she said to Mario, biting his lip sexily. "I'll see you at lunch?"

"I have to leave early today," he told her. "But I'll call you tonight, and we can talk more about tomorrow night, OK?"

"OK."


When Saturday came, Taina kept her word to her parents. She didn't say a word to them. She locked her bedroom door, and Stephanie was the only person she allowed to enter. She almost slipped up and told Stephanie about her plans for the night, but she didn't want to put her in that kind of situation. Instead, she kept it to herself. She hadn't told Marisol her plans because she didn't want her to know yet. Knowing Marisol, she would either try to talk her out of it or ask too many questions. Taina passed the time by watching TV and texting Marisol.

Isabella tried to come to have a girls' talk with Taina, but Taina would not open the door for her. She was now trying to be a real mother, but it was too late. The seed of resentment was already planted deeply in Taina's heart. Instead of answering the knocks on her door, she opted to turn up her TV loudly, showing her mother blatant disrespect.

*Fuck you,* Taina thought.

The rest of the day seemed to drag. She didn't know if it was because she looked at the clock every five minutes or because time was moving slowly. It took a lifetime for it to get to eleven o'clock finally. Then Taina took a shower and got dressed. She put on a pair of black leggings and opted for a black and red Chicago Bulls T-shirt for her shirt. As for her hair, she put it all on the top of her head in a messy bun. After she sprayed herself with her Victoria's Secret perfume, she slid on a pair of socks and stuck her feet into her red Ugg boots.

She opened her bedroom door and peeked out while silently putting on her coat. It was almost midnight, so she was betting her father wasn't home and her mother was in bed asleep. She looked down the hall and kicked herself when she saw the door open. The lights were off, though. The only light she could see was from the television, so maybe things would work in her favor.

Locking her door behind her, she shut it gently and checked her pocket to ensure she had the keys and her cell phone. Taina crept along the wall like a 9-year-old sneaking downstairs to eat some cookies. When she reached her parents' bedroom door, she peeked in the huge room. As she suspected, her father wasn't there, and her mother lay alone in the king-sized bed. That wasn't the best part. That night, her mother had decided to wear a mask that covered her eyes. Taina didn't take any chances; she hurried past the door and toward the stairs without looking back.

When she reached the main floor, she knew going out of the front door was not an option, so she continued walking until she reached the basement. Once there, she went to the cold laundry room and shut that door behind her. She looked for something she could stand on, and her eyes spotted the prize. She found a crate in the corner and pulled it over the concrete floor to the window she was going to use to make her escape. She stood atop the crate on her tiptoes to push the window open. As soon as she did, a huge gust of wind caught her by surprise, and she had to inhale deeply before she could keep going. She quickly shut the window again.

It was small, so Taina knew it would be a tight fit, but she didn't care. All she could think about was seeing Mario. She looked out the window, knowing that although none of her father's men were patrolling it, there was still a camera somewhere.

"There!" she said when she saw the rotating camera.

All she needed to do was time it just right. She counted the seconds in between its rotation and figured out that there was a seven-second window. The moment it started turning the other way, Taina hoisted herself through the window. She had to wiggle her butt hard to get it through, but it worked. Once she was outside, she made a run for it. She checked her phone and saw that it was just about midnight. There was a reason why she'd chosen that time. She knew that's when the night watch switched, and she also knew that they always left their post five minutes early before the next person came. Realizing that she only had a few minutes, she took out her phone and used an app to open the gate. She slid right on through and shut it back before it was even all the way opened.

She walked straight down the neighborhood, looking for Mario's car. Just when she thought he must have forgotten about her, she saw a car's headlights driving toward her. The Corvette pulled up beside her, and she heard the doors unlock. Without hesitation, she pulled the passenger door open and hopped in. Seeing Mario, she threw her arms around him and hugged him tightly.

"Wow," he said, admiring her. "You pulled it off."

Taina grinned proudly like the Cheshire cat and let him go so that she could put her seat belt on.

"Where are we going?" she asked.

"I got us a hotel suite not too far from here," Mario said. "So we won't have to be in the car the whole time."

"You think you're slick." Taina's eyes lowered, and she bit her lip.

He laughed.

"What?" He lifted the middle console and pulled out an already rolled blunt and a lighter.

"Stop talking shit and spark this."

"Gladly," she said.

When they arrived at the room Mario had reserved for them, they were both so high they could barely feel their feet touching the ground. Since Mario had already checked in, all they had to do was get on the elevator and go up to their room.

"Here," Mario gave Taina the room key so that she could open the door and enter first.

She did and was instantly filled with emotion. Rose petals surrounded the king-sized bed, and a bottle of Champagne chilled in ice on the nightstand beside it. On the bed were at least twenty miniature Snickers bars, her favorite chocolate, shaped into a heart.

"Oh, Mario." Her hand shot to her mouth. "Nobody has ever done anything like this for me before."

"Well, if you haven't ever gone on a regular date before, I wouldn't doubt that," he joked, and she playfully pinched his arm. He took off his coat and helped her remove hers. Throwing them on one of the chairs, he waved her to the bed. "Come on, have a glass of Champagne."

"You're only 18," Taina said, watching him pour her a glass. "How did you even get this stuff?"

"I have connections." Mario handed her the glass and poured his own. He lifted his glass in the air. "To us. May we always remain close no matter what happens."

"To us," Taina gushed and took the cup to the head.

She had smoked weed a lot and drank a little, but that was the first time she mixed the two. It was a pleasant feeling. Her body felt amazing when it was touched, and Mario let his fingers trail up and down her arms ever so lightly. The two lay on the bed staring at the ceiling, talking and laughing.

"Have you ever just wanted to run away and never look back?" Taina whispered, turning to face him.

She hadn't noticed how close they were until that very second. Her face was only inches away from his. She saw his lips twitch like he wanted to smile, but it showed as more of a grimace.

"Been there, done that," he said. "This is my new life now . . . You are my new life."

"Promise?" Taina's voice came out as more of a purr than a whisper, and Mario heard it.

He turned to his side so that he could face her. Nudging her nose with his, he placed his right hand on the back of her head.

"Promise," he said and pulled her lips to his.

The kiss was deep and passionate, and Taina heard herself moaning in his mouth. She pressed her chest against him to let him know it was OK if he wanted to touch them. Her hands roamed freely on his muscular body, and she felt herself growing moist between her legs each time their tongues intertwined. Mario's hand slid under her T-shirt and massaged her breasts through her bra. Taina's clit throbbed each time he pinched her nipple. Mario pulled away and looked Taina in the eyes.

"Are you sure you want this?"

Taina was too gone to tell him no. All she wanted was for him to make her feel good. So to answer his question, she sat up, took off her shirt, and unsnapped her bra. Mario licked his lips at the sight of her perky nipples.

"Lick them," she instructed.

Mario did as he was told. When she felt his tongue, her back arched. She had never felt something so marvelous in her life. He slid off her leggings and panties with the swiftness of a sex expert. Once he removed them, he planted kisses from her chest down to her thighs. She felt herself growing nervous, but she didn't tell him to stop. Instead, she opened her legs.

"Taina?" he asked, sitting back up to face her.

"Yes?"

"Are you sure about this?" he asked again.

"Yes. I want you."

He smiled and kissed her passionately again. When he pulled away from her, he admired her.

"You are so beautiful. Can I tell you something?"

"Anything," she whispered.

"I love you," Mario said to her. "Do you love me?"

"Yes."

He grinned before laying her down on the bed. He removed his clothes and got on top of her. She took a deep breath, and Mario noticed her nervousness.

"I'll be gentle, OK, mami?" he said, and Taina nodded. "It's going to hurt at first, but after that, it will feel good. Bite me, scratch me, or scream loud as hell. Do whatever you need to. Just don't tell me to stop, OK?"

"OK," Taina said, gripping his back and preparing herself.

Mario positioned himself at her opening and pushed his manhood inside of her. It was the most painful thing she'd ever felt, and she clenched her eyes shut. She didn't understand how people liked doing it. Her hands clawed his back as he shivered on top of her. She whimpered and tried to stomach the pain. Just as she was about to tell him to stop, the hurt began to subside, and she felt something else. Pleasure. Her body began to relax, and she started to enjoy the ride. Mario made love to her and treated her delicately for what felt like forever, but honestly, was only about five minutes. Soon, his body jerked, and he pulled himself out of her just as he ejaculated on the bed. They were both breathing heavily when he collapsed next to her. They scooted over to the side of the bed without the wet spots and cuddled closely.

Taina knew she could only sleep for a few hours before returning home, but that was OK. She had the best night ever. At that moment, a feeling of guilt came over her as she thought about her promise to her father so long ago.

"Welp," she said, "I can kiss that million goodbye."

"What's up?" Mario asked, but Taina just snuggled deeper into her man's chest.

"Nothing," she said. "Wake me up in three hours, baby."

# Chapter 8

Denny sat in his office study staring at the portrait he had drawn of his family when Taina was only 1 year old. He sat in a chair fit for a king with a smiling Taina sitting on his knee. Isabella stood behind him with her hands on her shoulders. If only he could go back to those days and start over. He sighed. The weekend had come and gone. Taina kept her word because she didn't say a thing to either of her parents. She avoided them at all costs, and he wasn't even sure if she had eaten. Maybe he should have just let her go on that date. He could have had his men follow them and watch her for him. Instead, he let his ego get the best of him, and he used his position of power against his daughter. He poured himself a shot of vodka. Then his cell phone vibrated, and he answered it before he took the drink to the head.

"Hello?"

"I'm about to kill your daughter," a gruff voice said on the other end.

"Who the fuck is this?" Denny demanded.

"You have much worse problems on your hands than knowing who I am," the voice said. "Right now, your daughter is walking to her lunch table in the cafeteria, holding her tray tightly. She's smiling. She doesn't have a clue that she's about to die."

"If you touch her, I'll—"

"You'll *what?* Star sixty-nine me? Ha! You're a played-out boss, and I'm about to show you what it feels like to take away somebody's loved one."

The caller hung up, and Denny didn't know if it was a prank call or what. Either way, he moved as fast as possible to round up his men and send them to his daughter's school before it was too late.

"You didn't talk to them at all?" Marisol said to Taina after they set their trays on the lunch table.

"Nope," Taina told her. "He didn't even have a real reason why I couldn't go. He was just trying to be controlling. I swear, I'm out of that house as soon as possible."

"You don't seem too angry, though," Marisol said, eyeballing her friend. "You've been smiling all day. What happened that you *aren't* telling me about?"

Taina's grin said it all. She didn't even have to say anything for Marisol to get it.

"Oh my goodness," Marisol exclaimed, pushing her tray out of her way. She suddenly lost her appetite. "Chica . . . Did you guys fuck?"

Taina nodded, still smiling like a maniac. Marisol stood up and went to the other side of the table to sit next to her. She grabbed her hands and looked into her eyes.

"How the fuck did you pull that off?"

"You know that small window in the basement at my house? I snuck out of it."

"You mean to tell me you got that big ass through that small-ass window?"

"Yes, girl. But the struggle was too real." They both laughed. "But no, seriously, that window is the only blind spot with the security guards. The camera will still pick it up, but I waited for it to rotate the other way. Mario was waiting down the street, and when I made it through the gate, we spent the rest of the night together. It was so amazing."

"Did it hurt?"

"Hell yes, it hurt. But it was a good pain, I guess."

The two girls talked about Taina losing her virginity for the rest of their lunch hour. Marisol told her she was proud that she'd finally taken a stand for herself. Finally, she looked at the lunch ladies and the new lunch guys helping them take the food back into the kitchen.

"I've never seen those guys before, have you?" Marisol asked, standing up to take her tray to the trash can.

Taina stood up with her tray and stared at the guys Marisol was talking about. There were four of them, and Taina instantly made a weird face.

"Why are there four of them? I didn't know the lunch ladies needed that much help."

The question hadn't even been out of her mouth for a full second when the men noticed Taina staring at them. There were two Black men, one white man, and one Hispanic. One of the white guys smiled sinisterly at Taina. All four men then threw their lunch attire over their heads, revealing black suits and automatic weapons. Taina saw it before it happened, but it was too late. She tried to grab Marisol when she took cover under their table in the cafeteria, but the bullets from the shooters ripped into Marisol's body, making her look like a dancing rag doll.

"Marisol!" Taina screamed repeatedly, holding on to her friend's body as they dropped to the floor.

Marisol tried to say something, but it sounded like a gurgle. Blood poured from her mouth, and Taina tried to apply pressure to her wounds. All around her, the multiple gunshots and the screaming of her fellow classmates faded into the background of her hearing. She was only focused on her best friend lying in her arms, choking on her blood. Marisol feverishly reached for Taina's hand and squeezed it tightly.

"I love you, Marisol. You are my very best friend," Taina whispered, letting her tears fall on Marisol's face.

Marisol gave her what was supposed to be a smile.

"I-I love y . . . you too. P . . . please don't f . . . forget me, OK?"

"I promise," Taina said.

Before Taina could say anything else, she felt Marisol's grip on her hand slacken and watched her opened eyes go dim. Taina let go of her hand and shut Marisol's eyes to make it look like she was sleeping. She put her friend's head to her chest and sobbed. She didn't care if a bullet caught her right then and there. The one person in the world who understood her was gone; it was like she was lying dead with her already. She shook and sobbed into Marisol's hair, silently praying for her to please come back. She didn't plan on letting her go until she felt a hand tightly grip her shoulder.

"Taina, we have to go!" Taina looked up to see Mario standing over her. "It's too late for Marisol, but we need to get out of here now. They came for you."

*They came for you.* His words echoed in her head.

The bullets that were made for her had gotten to Marisol instead. Taina kissed her forehead.

"I'm so sorry, Marisol," she whispered. "I'm so sorry."

"Come on, Taina! Your dad's men are here, but I don't know how long they can hold them off."

Taina finally listened to reason and laid Marisol's body down gently.

"I'll come back for you," Taina promised and struggled to her feet.

The two of them ran away from the gunfire as quickly as they could. Taina almost couldn't stomach the sight of the bloody bodies of students she kept stumbling across. Some were still alive, while others weren't so lucky.

"Aah!" Mario yelled as a bullet grazed his arm.

"Mario!" Taina cried out.

"I'm OK." Mario winced at the wound. "It just grazed me. Keep going. My car is in the back of the building."

They made it out of the building without any other occurrences and ran hand in hand to Mario's red Corvette. He put the key in the ignition and floored the gas pedal all the way to Taina's house. Right before they reached the gate, Taina asked Mario to pull over. She opened the passenger-side door and leaned out. Everything in her stomach rushed out, and she tried to catch her breath.

"Hey, hey." Mario rubbed her back.

He felt her long hair under his slender fingers as his hand went back and forth between her shoulder blades. Her heart thumped rapidly while she continued to take deep breaths. It wasn't until then that he noticed she was covered in blood, and her face was pale.

"Come on," Mario said. "Let's get you home. Your parents are probably really worried about you."

Taina nodded and shut her door. Mario drove up to the gate and saw an armed man standing there. He walked up to the driver's-side window, and Mario rolled it down.

"Can you please tell Mr. Capello that I have his daughter, Taina, with me?"

The guard's face registered surprise, and he looked over into the passenger's side. When he saw that it was, in fact, Taina, he opened the gate and waved them through. At the same time, he radioed to the house that Taina was home. Taina pointed Mario to her house. He helped her out of the car and up the steps that led up to the front door. Taina pushed it open, and she was bombarded with a swarm of people around her no sooner than she stepped into the house.

"Oh, thank God." Stephanie was the first person to embrace her. "I was so worried. Oh my God, she's covered in blood!"

"I . . . It's not mine," Taina was able to get out.

Isabella came forward and pulled Taina away from Stephanie to hug her daughter.

"I'm glad you're OK, baby," she said into Taina's hair. "We got the call that somebody was shooting at the school, and we thought the worst. Your father is on his way back here now."

Taina pulled away and just nodded her head. She was numb all over. All she wanted to do was go to her room and sleep. Maybe it would have all just been one horrible nightmare when she woke up. Everyone around her began overwhelming her with a million questions. The only one she heard was Stephanie's.

"If that isn't your blood, Taina, whose is it?"

Taina's eyes welled with tears again, and her bottom lip trembled. She opened her mouth to speak but couldn't find the words. The image of Marisol lying lifeless in the school's cafeteria entered her head, and it was too much for her to bear for one day.

"I think she's been through enough today," Mario finally said from behind them.

Suddenly, all eyes turned to where the strange voice had come from.

"Who are you?" Isabella asked. "What is he doing here?"

"My name is—"

"Taina!" Denny Capello's voice boomed throughout the house when he pushed the door open and saw his daughter standing there.

He left his security guards outside the house and rushed to swoop her off the ground. He held her tightly to him like a baby and kissed her face. He studied her from top to bottom when he put her back down.

"You have blood all over you," he observed. "Are you all right?"

"It's not my blood," Taina said, struggling with her speech. "It's . . . It's Marisol's. She's dead," she sobbed.

She was finally able to say it, and Stephanie gasped. She had to sit. Stephanie then knew why Taina's face was so pale. Her best friend had been murdered right before her eyes. From the looks of it, Taina must have held her until the end.

"No," she exclaimed. "Oh Lord, not Marisol."

"Papi," Taina said, looking up into Denny's eyes, "is it true that those men came looking for me today? Is it true that they wanted to kill me?"

Instead of answering, Denny looked to Isabella for help. She came and stood by his side. Gripping his hand, she tried to talk to Taina.

"Honey—"

"They *did* mean to kill me," Taina screamed. "But they killed Marisol instead. But they were trying to kill *me*."

Taina was hysterical by then. Her sobs were uncontrollable, and she looked at both of her parents with deep anger.

"Taina—" Her mother tried again. This time, she reached for Taina, but Taina threw her hand away.

"Fuck you!" she screamed. "This is all *his* fault!" She pointed a finger at her father. "My best friend is dead. She's dead, and she's not coming back." Taina had to take a breath. Then she backed away until she reached the stairs leading to her bedroom. Her face was completely twisted, and she cried like a 5-year-old. "I hate you! I don't want to live like this anymore! I have lost the only person in this world that ever truly gave a fuck about me, and you can stand there nonchalant as hell like *I'm* not the one with blood on my body?"

With that, she turned and ran up the stairs leaving all of them standing there in awkward silence. Stephanie nodded her respects to Mario for bringing her home safely and ran up the stairs after her. Denny wiped his face with his hand and tried to understand what had just happened.

When he and his men had arrived at the scene, the shooters were already dead. He couldn't understand why they had even gone to the trouble of invading the school in the first place. The first person that came to his mind was Rodriguez, but although Denny had pretty much taken over his operation by force, Rodriguez still had a major hand in all the dealings. He was making more money in the heroin game being partnered with Denny than he ever had running things solo. So until he figured out exactly what was going on and who called the hit, he would need to double his security.

Marisol's death deeply saddened him. He knew how close she and Taina had been. She was the first real friend Taina ever had that didn't use her for the perks of having a wealthy friend. However, he would have been lying if he said he wasn't glad it was her and not Taina.

Denny finally noticed the tall boy standing in the room with them. He'd been so relieved to see Taina home alive and safe that he hadn't even seen the stranger in his home. Denny could tell he was trying to decide whether to leave or go upstairs after Taina. From the concerned look in his eyes, he guessed that this was the boy his daughter had begged to go on a date with.

"Mario," Denny said, catching the boy off guard.

"Yes, sir, Mr. Capello, sir," Mario stammered.

"I was told that you were the one who rescued my daughter and brought her home," Denny said, walking to Mario and standing directly before him. "Is that true?"

"Yes."

Denny sized up Mario and then finally nodded his head. Finally, he held out his hand for Mario to shake.

"Thank you," Denny said. "I apologize that you had to witness that."

"No problem at all," Mario said, shaking his hand. "I'm just glad she's OK. If it's all right with you, I would like to check on her before I leave."

Denny contemplated the boy's words. He knew that the right thing to do was allow him to go upstairs and console his daughter, especially since his face was probably one of the only ones she could stomach at the moment. Denny waved his hand to the stairs.

"I might have been wrong about you," Denny said, remembering how hard he'd been on his daughter's crush. "Go on. When you come back down, my security will let you out. I have some business to attend to."

"Thank you, sir," Mario said and hurried past him.

Halfway up the stairs, Denny Capello surprised him again.

"And Mario?" Denny said.

"Yes, sir?"

"Come on over on Sunday. I would be honored if you joined us for dinner."

Mario was shocked, but instead of showing it, he flashed Denny the best smile he could muster, given the grimness of the situation.

"I would love to."

# Chapter 9

Taina was allowed to skip school the for rest of the week. She couldn't find the strength to get up and return to that school. All she had been thinking about was Marisol. Her family had laid her to rest only two days after, and the funeral was hard to attend, but she went and sat in the front with the rest of Marisol's family. She could say her final goodbyes to her best friend, and although she was sure Marisol was at peace, she wasn't. Her heart ached because she knew that Marisol was dead, and it was all her fault. If she hadn't been friends with Taina in the first place, she wouldn't have been sitting at that lunch table and would still be alive. She thought of all the times they shared and looked through all the selfies they'd taken on her phone. Spring was around the corner, and she couldn't believe she would bring in her eighteenth birthday without her best friend.

Taina cried every day after the funeral and stayed locked in her room. She didn't eat; she just lay there feeling sick. The only thing that provided her solace was that her father had invited Mario over for dinner on Sunday. She knew he only did that because he felt guilty for ruining her life, but she would take it. The only other person that she thought she had left in the world was Mario. She had distanced herself from everyone, including Stephanie. The only person who heard her voice was her boyfriend.

When Sunday night finally came, she showered and combed her hair. She dressed and wore a pretty cream-colored dress and a pair of brown flats. Her hair flowed around her shoulders. Finally, she opened her bedroom door to show her face to the rest of the household. She smelled the amazing aroma from the kitchen as her mother and the cooks made of all their favorite traditional foods, and she heard her father and his friends in the living room watching some sports game. Things had been tense around the home since the shooting, and her father had more security around than usual. But it was nice to feel the ambiance of their sacred family Sundays again.

Taina told Mario to be there at eight, and at seven fifty, the doorbell rang. She beat the housekeeper to the door and flung it open. Sure enough, on the other side of the door was her boo holding a bouquet of roses. He smiled at her when he saw her.

"Wow, you look amazing," he said, handing her the flowers.

"Thank you. You do too," Taina said, taking in the black designer suit he chose to wear that night.

The two sneaked a quick kiss, and then she led him into the foyer.

"Just the person I wanted to see!" Denny said, coming from up behind the two teenagers. "Come sit down. The food is ready."

He took them into the dining room, where the long table was almost filled with food and people surrounding it. Denny sat at the head of the table with Taina to his left and Isabella to his right. Mario sat on the other side of Taina and ignored the curious stares he was receiving from everyone at the table. He was there for one reason and one reason only: not to mingle with the likes of them.

Taina grabbed his hand under the table, and he smiled at her. Like always, Denny requested everyone to bow their heads as he prayed before anyone dug into the food.

"So, Mario, my daughter tells me you are in the same grade as her at school?" Isabella said after everyone had loaded up their plates.

"Yes, I am, Mrs. Capello," he answered, swallowing a forkful of rice.

"What are your plans after graduation?"

"I hope to go to a college on the West Coast so I can study to become an architect," he answered with a smile.

Isabella nodded, seemingly pleased with his response. Everyone else was engaged in their conversations, but Denny and Isabella focused more on Mario. Denny didn't know what it was, but there was something about Mario that he recognized from somewhere. However, he was sure that he'd never seen him before.

"Do you have any family here in Manhattan?" Denny asked, taking a couple of bites of his food.

"I live with my aunt and uncle here," Mario told him. And before Denny could ask, he said, "My parents died when I was a little kid. Dad died in a car accident, and my mother died when I was 10. Cancer."

"I'm so sorry," Isabella said, her voice dripping with sympathy. "Well, I'm glad your family took you in so you didn't have to jump from house to house."

"Tell me about it," Mario said. "Can you imagine my Hispanic ass being raised in foster care? I'd definitely have fallen into every single stereotype."

Even Denny laughed at that, and Taina felt herself relaxing. The dinner went without a hitch, and everyone was getting along just fine. Taina even found herself smiling and being nice to her mother. When dinner was over, all their guests left except for Mario. Denny whisked him off to show him around the house, leaving the two women behind to clean off the table and wash the dishes.

"He seems nice," Isabella said to her daughter. "You like him a lot, huh?"

"Yeah, I do," Taina said, drying the dishes in the dish drainer. "He's an amazing person."

"I remember when I first met your father," Isabella said dreamily. "I remember the feeling he gave me and the first time we—"

"Mommy!" Taina exclaimed and put her wet hands to her ears.

Isabella giggled like a schoolgirl.

"Well, I'm just saying. That man is something else," she said. Suddenly, she sighed. "Taina, I know we haven't had the best relationship since you've entered your teenage years. And now, with Marisol gone and you about to leave home soon, I would like to fix that. I don't want to lose you."

Taina pondered over her words for a few moments and was tempted to tell her to go shove them up her ass. But she knew that being bitter wouldn't help the situation, either, so instead of being mean, she nodded.

"OK, Mommy, I won't say that it will be an overnight thing. But I will try if you do."

Isabella cocked her head and touched her daughter's cheek. She sometimes didn't think she had anything to do with her daughter's being there. The only thing Taina got from Isabella was her physique and her high cheekbones. Other than that, she was her father's child completely. They made small talk and laughed together for a few more moments before Taina left to find her father and boyfriend.

"I'll be right back, Mommy," she said, handing her mother the kitchen towel.


Denny led Mario upstairs to his study and shut the double doors behind them. He then lit a Cuban cigar and handed it to Mario, who took it and puffed a little too hard. He broke into a coughing fit, and Denny patted his back, finding humor in Mario's struggle.

"You need more practice," Denny said, taking the cigar back from him.

"It looks that way, huh?" Mario said and wiped the tears from his eyes. "I think I'll give myself a few more years before I try that again."

Denny went and sat behind his desk. He blew on his cigar and motioned for Mario to sit across from him. When Mario sat down, the two men looked at each other.

"What are your intentions with my daughter, Mario?" Denny asked the question he didn't want to ask when Taina was around. He knew she would throw a fit and didn't feel like hearing her mouth.

"My intentions with Taina are to make her happy," Mario answered smoothly.

"And how do you plan on doing that?"

"By doing everything everyone else around her has failed to do."

Denny was taken aback by the boldness of the kid. He just took another drag of his cigar without saying anything. He was impressed, and he was about to give Mario his blessing, but Mario cut him off with these threatening words:

"OK." Mario laughed evilly. He put his elbows on the desk and leaned in. "Enough with the charades. I'm not here to get your blessing to date your daughter, Denny. I'm not even here for her. I came for you."

"Excuse me?" Denny asked, not sure if he'd heard him right.

"Exactly what I said. I came for you," Mario said, pulling a pistol from his waist. "Your biggest mistake tonight was letting me enter your home without your security checking me. Put your gun on the table, and we can talk."

Mario pointed his weapon at Denny's head, but Denny sat unmoving, staring into Mario's evil eyes.

"I am in my home," Denny said. "I am unarmed."

Mario kept his gun aimed at Denny's head and went to the other side of the desk to check to see if he was being lied to. When he was sure Denny had no weapon, he made Denny switch seats.

"How does it feel?" Mario asked. "To know you've been tricked. You let me walk right in."

"Why don't you tell me who you are?" Denny said, his voice still even.

The gun pointed at his head did not intimidate him. However, it bothered him that he had no clue who the person before him was.

*Who has my daughter allowed in my house?* he asked himself.

"Look at me," Mario demanded. "Tell me, who do you see?"

Denny couldn't say. He looked familiar, but he couldn't put his finger on why.

"You don't know, do you? With as many bodies as you must have under your belt, it's hard to remember one from years ago, huh?" Mario shook his head.

"You just said that you were done with the charades," Denny said in a bored tone. "But it seems to me that you're still playing them. I don't do guessing games."

"Diablo!" Mario screamed in Denny's face. "You killed my uncle."

Denny's mouth opened slightly, but he quickly shut it. It all made sense to him now. Mario looked so much like Diablo that he could have smacked himself for not making the connection. It had just been so long since he had seen Diablo's face. He had heard of the past coming back to hurt him, and Denny was a sure believer in Karma, but he always thought he could outrun his, especially since he had just wrapped up such a large business deal.

"Your uncle was robbing me," Denny said.

"Because you weren't paying him enough money," Mario screamed.

It was all coming out. Ever since Mario had come to New York, he had a plan. He lied to Taina when he told her he lived with his aunt and uncle. The truth was somebody named "Tommy" Rodriguez had put a high price on Denny Capello's head. Denny was positioned to seize control of most of Rodriguez's business, and he couldn't have that. He'd come seeking help from Mario's only living uncle, Carlos, to exact revenge, but Carlos had long since left the life of being an assassin behind him. He had come to peace with the deaths of his brother and sister, and he didn't need death knocking on his door any sooner than it was supposed to. By eavesdropping, Mario discovered the truth about what really happened to his mother and uncle. Since his uncle would not avenge their deaths, he decided he would. Rodriguez told him that Capello had a daughter his age and that to get to Denny, he would need to get to her.

Mario enrolled in the same school as Taina Capello, but he never bet on her being as beautiful and down-to-earth as she was. He never bet on genuinely falling for her, but his mission was more important. What had happened in the cafeteria was his doing as well. He let Rodriguez know that Denny did not have any men inside the school, only outside. Rodriguez sent his soldiers disguised as lunch helpers to start a massacre in the middle of her lunch period. It all was a ploy to make Mario look like a hero. Even the graze on his arm was staged. He never meant for Taina's best friend to get killed, but there were casualties in all wars. Taina was already so broken, and it pained him to hurt her even more, but he would move on and never look back after he finished there. Taina would be a memory, and his new girlfriend would be a hefty bank account.

"Diablo was trying to take care of his family," Mario yelled again. "His sister, my mother, was dying, and all they needed was one more payment to start a more aggressive medical procedure for her. But that payment never came because you had him killed. You killed Uncle Diablo, and you killed my mother. So I fucked your daughter, and now, I will kill you."

Mario applied pressure to the trigger but couldn't get a shot off because Denny reached over and knocked the gun out of his hand. Denny caught him with a right hook so hard that Mario felt like an earthquake was occurring in the room. But Mario recovered quickly and came back at Denny with a combination of power punches to his gut. Where Denny excelled in power, Mario had speed. To every powerful blow that Denny landed, Mario landed three. Unknown to Denny, Mario had a knife in his belt as well. Denny went to slam Mario on the ground, but while holding him in midair, Mario retrieved the knife and shoved it into Denny's chest.

"Aah!" Denny cried out in pain and dropped Mario to the ground.

He staggered back and yanked the knife from his chest. He put his massive hand over the wound, but it was no help. Blood gushed through his fingers and dripped on his clean carpet, staining it. Denny's breathing was short. He fell to the ground with his back on his desk. He tried to reach for the phone in his pocket. All he had to do was hit one button for his security to sweep the building clean and save him, but a kick to his temple stopped any feeble attempt at a rescue.

"The fuck do you think you're doing?" Mario had gotten back to his feet.

His face had started to swell with the hits Denny had landed there. Mario again had the gun in his hand and pointed it at Denny. He almost laughed at how easy it all had been. The sight of Denny's blood and defeat made Mario feel powerful.

"Any last words?" Mario panted, aiming the gun at the spot between Denny's eyes.

Denny sat there awaiting death, ready for it. He realized then that nothing had been Taina's fault. It was his. It all was his fault. That was his only regret in life.

"T-tell Taina that it wasn't her fault," Denny told Mario. "Don't let her live with this grief on her soul. T-tell her I always loved her."

Mario nodded his head.

"Sure, old man. Rodriguez sends his love."

The loud bang of the gun filled the room.

# Chapter 10

Blood. All Taina saw was the blood. The smile once plastered on Taina's face vanished when she slid open the doors to her father's study. All the laughter in her chest washed away only to be replaced with a searing pain by the sight she saw. There lay the notorious Denny Capello on his back with his eyes still wide open, and he had a neat red dot between his eyes. Taina caught herself on the door handle and slapped her hand to her mouth to stifle whatever sound dared to escape her lips. Her breathing was short and quick as her eyes darted around the room, looking for the intruder. The only thing her eyes saw was an open window, and the particles from the back of her father's head plastered on everything behind him.

"Papi," Taina croaked finally. Her voice was barely audible. "Papi!"

Her whole body shook violently, and she dropped to the ground. Her tongue tasted salt, and she realized tears slid down her face and landed inside her quivering mouth. She crawled from the entrance of the study to her father's lifeless body. As she crawled, her dress got stained with his blood. She shook him when she reached his body, hoping he would wake up, but his eyes held the same dull look that Marisol's had. He was gone. Taina got up and turned to run, but she ran right into Stephanie and her mother.

"Taina, what's wrong? And what's all that noise from your father's study?" Stephanie asked.

"It's Papi. He's-he's—"

"What's wrong with your father?" Isabella asked. She barely gave Taina a second glance as she walked past her. Stephanie looked at Taina's heartbroken face, and curiosity filled her. "Honey, we heard a lot of commo—" Isabella started, but when she saw the scene before her, she almost had a heart attack. "Oh God, no."

She gasped, seeing her husband lying there dead. Stephanie peered into the room in disbelief, pressing Taina's face against her face to shield her from the sight. But it was too late. She'd already seen her father's dead body. Isabella dropped to the ground and crawled just as Taina had toward Denny's body.

"Baby." She shook him. "Denny! No, no, no. You promised you wouldn't leave me. Please, baby, wake up."

Stephanie stared on in horror, but she was able to radio the security downstairs to check the perimeters of their property for the culprit. She couldn't believe it. Denny Capello was dead. Suddenly, she thought of something. She had seen Denny and Mario enter Denny's study alone after dinner. Maybe he saw something.

"Taina," Stephanie said, snapping the girl out of her deep trance. "Taina, where is Mario?"

Taina wasn't in a position to answer any questions, but the security guard who had just entered the room was able to give them an answer.

"He just left not even five minutes ago," the guard said. "He looked dinged up like he got into a fight."

"He did this!" Isabella screamed while she sobbed. "He killed my husband. Oh my God, he killed my husband. Denny! Denny!"

The remainder of the night was a blur. When the paramedics arrived, Denny Capello was pronounced dead on arrival. Isabella threw her body on the stretcher, not wanting them to take her husband away.

Chris arrived not too long after and couldn't believe his eyes. His cousin was dead. At first, he thought it was a joke, not believing anybody could take out an ox like Denny, but when he saw it for himself, he knew it was true. The first thing he did was speak to the police officers and federal agents, who were glad to have a reason to come snooping around Denny's residence. Taina and Isabella went with them to fill out a report, and Chris sent the rest of them on their way after all the pictures of the murder scene were taken.

Once the coast was clear, he went to Denny's recording console in the house. Denny had his home and neighborhood on at least twenty TV video screens for surveillance. He played back the video of what had happened in Denny's study that night and witnessed Taina's boyfriend killing Denny. He also heard everything he said to Denny, including when Mario was about to pull the trigger and said that Rodriguez had sent him. Chris turned off the recording. He bet that Rodriguez thought nobody would discover that Denny was killed under his order. Chris also bet that Denny had a feeling the deal with Rodriguez might turn foul and had a spy in Rodriguez's camp ready to pull the trigger on call. He took out his phone and dialed a number.

"Pull the plug and bleed that whole motherfucking thing dry. The Eagle is down. Plans have changed."

# Chapter 11

Attending the funeral of her father was not something Taina planned on doing so soon. She was lost. Her best friend was already six feet under, and her father would be soon. Taina walked up the pews with her mother a few steps ahead of her and tried to avoid the stares of those around them. She heard somebody whisper the word "devil" when she walked by, and Taina had to pretend she heard nothing. Knowing that the whole community blamed her for her father's death hurt her heart. Even her mother showed some resentment toward her. She was glad the veil from her hat covered the tears sliding down her face.

Denny had a glorious homegoing. Chris made sure he sat beside Taina. He had heard Denny's final request. Although everyone was making her feel like she wasn't worth two nickels rubbed together, he wanted her to know that she was the last thought on his mind before he died. He held her hand during the entire service and allowed her to ride to the grave site with him.

Taina kept her head down and stayed back while everyone else threw their roses onto the casket when it was lowered into the earth. When everyone left, Taina slowly walked to the coffin. She kissed her white rose and sent a silent prayer to her father. She hoped that he was at peace wherever his soul rested, and she apologized for bringing evil into his home. With one last goodbye, she threw her rose onto the casket containing her father's body.

"I love you, Papi," she whispered into the wind chill. "Always."

Chris came behind her and threw his rose on the casket as well. After that, he put his arm around her and hugged her.

"Come on, princess. Let me get you home," he said.

"What home?" Taina asked, shrugging her shoulders. "My mother hates me."

"She doesn't hate you."

"She does," Taina said, her voice shaky. "She won't look at me. And when she does, I can see it in her eyes."

Chris didn't know what to say because, knowing the type of attitude Isabella had, Taina was probably telling the truth. Instead of trying to console Taina, she most likely was shunning her like she'd done even when Denny was still alive. Since she'd saved his life, Chris had always felt a closeness with Taina. He knew that her heart was kind, and this was something she wouldn't have wished on anyone. He knew that how she thought and acted resulted from her upbringing, but Isabella would never take responsibility for that.

"Come on," Chris urged. "We will visit his burial site often."

Taina followed him back to his Mercedes-Benz and got in the passenger seat. Before they pulled away, Taina asked her cousin a question.

"Do you think Papi hates me?"

"Never, my love," Chris told her. "Denny loved you with all that he had. If anything, he is hoping from his grave that *you* don't hate *him*. I am now in charge of all your father's business, and the person who ordered the hit won't even have a funeral. I want you to know that regardless of whatever happens, you will be set for life. I'm leaving New York. With your father gone, there is nothing left for me here. But if you ever need me for anything, just call me. I will never change my number."

With that, he pulled off from the cemetery and let the others pay their respects. He nodded his head at the hired hands he had guarding his cousin's grave site, making sure that nobody would come and be disrespectful. He drove Taina back home and kissed her on her forehead.

"I love you, princess," Chris said.

"I love you too, Chris," Taina said, trying to smile at him.

It was weak, but he was happy that she could even muster up that one. She waved her final farewell to Chris Capello and walked into the house. When she entered, she saw many people there. All Taina saw was black; she just wanted to make it to her bedroom. When she was spotted, some people stopped their speech, letting her know they were most likely discussing her. She saw many people surrounding her mother, and when Isabella's eyes fell on Taina's, her nose flared in disgust.

"Get her out of my face," Taina heard her say as she pointed in her daughter's direction.

"I will not allow you to speak to her that way," Taina heard Stephanie say in her defense. "If you would have been a mother instead of a credit card user, then maybe none of this would have happened, bitch."

"You're fired," Isabella countered, but Stephanie just laughed.

"We all know that when Denny died, he left everything to Chris and Taina. You can't fire shit."

Taina ignored their argument and ran upstairs to her room. When she got there, she broke down in a fit of screams. She cried for her father, Marisol, and the fact that the boy she had fallen in love with had betrayed her. Taina had tried to call Mario many times, but his phone was disconnected. She didn't know where he lived. She never inquired where he laid his head at night the whole time they talked. She felt like a fool and didn't have anything to live for anymore. She threw off her hat and veil and lay across the floor.

The images of Marisol and her father's dull eyes entered her head. Her heart wrenched. She felt like she didn't deserve to breathe the air she was breathing. Struggling to her feet, Taina made her way to her panty drawer. From it, she pulled a small bottle of 1800 Tequila. Alcohol in hand, she went into the bathroom. Her eyesight was blurry, and she could barely see where she was going, but she knew what she was aiming for. When she was in the bathroom, she stared into the mirror on her medicine cabinet and saw the mascara running down her face. Her lip trembled when she looked at her face. All she saw was her father.

"Fuck!" she screamed and punched the mirror.

The glass shattered, and blood from her wounded hand dripped into the sink. She ignored the pain in her hand and opened the cabinet, looking for something—anything. Her hand fell on a bottle of Tylenol, so she popped open the top. She didn't use any water, just alcohol, and she took the whole bottle to the head and swallowed.

It didn't take long for her to feel the drugs take effect. Taina dropped to the ground and watched as the world she knew faded around her. She was happy to leave a place where she had absolutely nothing and join Marisol and her father.

She last remembered seeing Stephanie's plump frame entering her room and calling her name. She screamed when she saw Taina lying on the ground and the open bottle of pills lying next to her.

# Chapter 12

*Three Years Later*

"Be strong. I love you, ladies!" a heartfelt voice said.

"I love you too!" Taina's voice sounded, and she welcomed the feeling of her friend's warm arms around her.

It had been three years since she attempted suicide, and what a journey it had been. Stephanie had found her on the floor, almost dead, and she was rushed to the hospital. They were able to resuscitate her, pump her stomach, and once she was well enough, they sent her to an institute to get better. It was a ride, but that was where she met Jay and Mila. They too were survivors of suicide attempts, and Taina was grateful for them.

Jay was a little rough around the edges, but she was loyal. She was Black and wore her natural curls down and around her face. Mila was mixed, but she was so light you would never be able to tell. After they finished their time at the facility, they remained friends. They were out celebrating three years of being alive after suicide attempts.

Taina's wounds were still fresh, and she couldn't be around her family. Seeing them might cause her to relapse, so she hadn't even tried to in three years. Sometimes she wondered if it was her deciding not to have a relationship, though. Her mother never reached out. Taina tried not to let it affect her and was just glad she'd made bonds with women as great as Jay and Mila. She smiled at Mila's big belly and rubbed it.

"You need to get home. You look so tired."

"I am. And there's Frank. I'll call when I get home," Mila said, giving them another hug.

Taina watched as she left the restaurant front and walked to the awaiting Toyota Camry of her husband. When she was gone, Taina turned to Jay, who was texting feverishly on her phone.

"You good?"

"Yeah, I'm just telling this asshole I'll be there after I take you home," Jay answered.

"Mami, just go. I'll catch a ride. I don't want you to miss your date with the new flavor of the week."

"Girl, you are more important than some dick."

"Well, I say, choose the dick," Taina laughed. "I'm a big girl. I'll be fine. Go."

"Taina . . ." Jay gave her a worried look.

"Go. I'll call you when I get home."

"As soon as you get home. Promise?"

"I promise."

"All right. I love you. See you later."

Taina waved and blew a kiss at Jay as she walked to where she had parked her car. Then Jay got in and drove away. Still smiling, Taina stepped toward a curb to hail a cab. Moments later, a yellow car pulled up. Once she got in the back, she gave the driver her address and leaned back in her seat. She stared out of the window, full of good Mexican food and ready to go to sleep.

"You look different, Taina," the driver said.

His voice was so familiar. She sat up straight and looked at him. He looked like . . . No, it couldn't be. She took another look at him, and her eyes widened.

"Mario?" She hadn't seen him in so long that she didn't know whether to be happy or sad. "What are you doing here?"

"Working," he said and chuckled. "I was sent to collect you."

"Collect me? What are you talking about?"

"You'll see."

She didn't like how he said that. Too much wasn't making sense to her. She hadn't seen him in three years, and then he magically popped up driving a taxi?

"How . . . How did you know where to find me?"

"I've been following you, waiting to get the okay."

"The okay? For what? Mario, you're not making sense." He didn't answer. He just continued driving. "If you aren't going to tell me what you're talking about, let me out. Let me out now."

She started banging on the window of the car. Something told her that she wasn't safe. She unlocked the door and prepared to jump out—but it didn't open. It was on child lock. Mario pulled the car over and slammed on the brakes. He turned to face her, and she saw a look in his eyes she didn't remember being there. They were as cold as ice.

"I had to wait for the okay to kill you."

He quickly sprayed something on her face that numbed her body when it went up her nostrils. She felt herself get hazy right before passing out completely.


"Wakey, wakey, Sleeping Beauty."

The voice sounded far away, and Taina could barely feel the slaps to her face. But when she came to, she recognized the familiar setting of her bedroom. She tried to get up, but she was so weak that she couldn't move. She also noticed that she was in nothing but her bra and underwear with her hands tied. She wished it was a nightmare, but she knew it wasn't when she saw Mario standing over her, holding a gun. Tears welled in her eyes.

"Why are you doing this?" she asked, sobbing lightly.

"Your mother's request," he answered simply.

"W-what? You're lying. And my mother hates you."

She didn't believe a word of what he said. She hadn't spoken to her mother in years. Why would she send anyone to hurt her?

"Aah." Mario smiled at her and kissed her chin. "You would think so, right? Since I killed your father, I got a pretty decent position as a top assassin in the underground. When your cousin Chris killed Rodriguez for having Denny killed, I thought I was a goner. But he kept me around because I'm useful."

"You're lying. He would have killed you before working with you."

"I'm not. He and your mother have long since forgotten about loyalty to your father. She is now on the arm of your dear cousin Chris."

"She wouldn't do that to Papi." Taina choked back her tears. "She wouldn't."

"But she would," Mario whispered in a singsong voice. "In fact, *they're* the ones who ordered the hit on you."

"No. Cousin Chris loves me," Taina said, not wanting to believe anything Mario said. Her head still throbbed, and she didn't have the strength to push him off her. "If anybody loves me, I know he does."

"I'm sure he does love you, but he loves money more," Mario said, wiggling his pants down. "At first, they had access to Denny's money and assets. But now that Denny's amended will has surfaced, it's come to light that Denny left everything to you. Everything was seized, and your mother's bank accounts were frozen. The only way she can get everything back is if you die. So . . . that's why I'm here. You have $200,000 on your head, and I plan on cashing in on that."

"Mario, you don't have to do this," she pleaded. "If my father's money is mine, I-I'll pay you double not to do this."

He stared at her for a long time, and she hoped he was contemplating her offer. But she knew it wasn't likely once the sinister smile spread on his face. He pulled a gun from his hip and aimed it at the center of her forehead.

"I was going to have some fun with you before I put you out of your misery, but not anymore. I gave your father the choice of having last words," he hissed. "But you? You won't get that pleasure."

When the shot rang out, Taina tensed up, waiting for the pain to come . . . but it never came. Instead, she felt Mario's heavy body fall on her and something warm dripping on her face. With wide eyes, she looked at him and could see the back of his head had been blown off. She squealed and pushed him off her with her weak arms.

"And this is why I carry a gun in my purse. I told you to call me when you got home."

Taina had never been happier to hear Jay's voice. She looked and saw her friend standing in the doorway with a smoking gun in her hand. Tears were in her eyes, and she ran to Taina.

"Y-you killed him," Taina said.

"He's not the first body on my belt. I had a rough childhood. Oh my God, Taina, are you okay?" she said, pushing Mario's lifeless body to the floor.

"I-I-I'm OK," Taina said, staggering to her feet, only to fall into Jay's arms. "He-he was going to kill me. How did you know to come?"

"Because you *always* call me when you get home. And today, you didn't. I don't know . . . Something just told me to come by. I felt like something was wrong."

Jay helped Taina walk out of the room and into her living room. She turned on a lamp and put Taina down gently on the couch. Sitting beside her, she examined Taina's bruised face. Jay shook her head sadly and embraced Taina tightly, trying not to cry. She thought the nightmare was over, but unfortunately, it was not for Taina. She just sat there staring into space with her head on Jay's shoulder.

"Who is he?" Jay said into Taina's hair.

"My ex-boyfriend," Taina told her. "The one who murdered my father."

"Word?" Jay asked with wide eyes. She pulled away from Taina and had a shocked expression on her face. "Why is he here? And how did he find you?"

"My mother and my cousin sent him to kill me," Taina told her, and Jay looked even more lost. "And I don't know how he found me. But I know that they won't stop until I'm dead. My father left everything he owned to me. And until I'm dead, it will remain that way."

"Fuck," Jay said. "I need to call Mila. She has connections."

"No," Taina exclaimed. "She and Frank are happy. Let them stay that way. We don't want to put stress on her and the babies. This was my fight before I knew you guys. I need to finish it alone."

Taina pushed away from Jay and struggled her way to the bathroom. All she wanted to do was shower. She ran hot water and realized there was no way to escape her past. She would have to face it. They would keep sending assassins to finish the job if they wanted her dead. She knew she would never be safe.

When she got out of the shower, she wiped her hand across the mirror and saw the girl who had once been so beautiful and innocent. She saw the girl who swallowed a bottle of pills, but she also saw the *woman* who had gotten through it all and cut the ribbon to the doors of her new company, ABC, with her newfound best friends. They were all the same person, and if she kept letting the past haunt her, she would never get past it. There was one voice that filled her heart that she needed closure from. She knew she would end the cycle by handling that bit of business.

When she opened the door with her towel around her, she saw Jay standing there with fresh clothes she handed over. Behind Jay, Taina saw a bag of her belongings that her friend had already packed.

"I packed your shit for you," Jay said. "Some of the shit might not match, but that's the least of our worries."

"Jay, you can't—"

"I can't *what?*" Jay cut her off. "Come with you? Regardless of whether you like it, Taina, you're my sister now. And I'm not going to let you dive into a suicide mission by yourself, a'ight?"

Taina knew Jay wouldn't take no for an answer, so she nodded. She gave Jay a small smile and embraced her. Wherever Marisol was, Taina was sure she was happy that she had finally made some real friends.

"OK, Jay," Taina said. "You win. Let me get dressed, and then I need you to help me figure out how we'll get this body out of my house."

Jay and Taina watched the car burn in an empty parking lot. They had started the fire.

"Bitch, I just burned up my car for you," Jay said, staring at the corpse in the front seat burning along with the leather of her foreign whip. "So you know I love you."

The two women threw their jacket hoods over their heads. They walked away from the scene like they had nothing to do with the flames burning behind them. When they got to the street where the cabdriver they had paid off to follow them was, they heard the explosion behind them. The fire had finally reached the gas tank.

"Goodbye, Mario," Taina said, looking back once more before she got into the backseat of the vehicle. "And fuck you very much."

"OK, now that that is done, what's our plan of action?"

Taina had told Jay everything that Mario had told her when he thought he would kill her. Jay shook her head at how grimy the world could be. She knew Taina had a touchy life, but she never guessed it was as bad as it was. Taina leaned back in her seat and felt the hatred buried deeply in her heart. It was time to show what Denny Capello's daughter was *really* made of.

"News of Mario's death will likely travel fast, especially since I am still alive and the only heir to my father's empire. I need to gun for them before they come after me again," Taina said, and Jay nodded, agreeing with her friend. "I think it's time I show my face at my childhood home. In Manhattan."

The drive to Manhattan didn't take very long, and although Taina was ready to kill right away, she knew she was in no shape to walk into what could have been a battlefield. She needed time to formulate a plan, and she was glad Jay was there to help her. They made the taxi driver drop them off at a hotel, the same Marriot that Mario had taken her to so long ago.

The two girls stayed up all night, trying to think of something. Jay made a few calls and got some throwaway guns dropped off to them. Taina palmed her pistol and asked herself if she was prepared to kill her mother.

"It's either them or you," Jay said, doing sit-ups on the floor. "If you don't do this, they will keep gunning for you like you said."

"I know," Taina replied.

"And if the security around that house is as tight as you say it is, then there is no getting through without being seen."

"Not helping," Taina groaned.

"I'm just being realistic," Jay said. "We should have just called Mila."

Jay's phone vibrated, and she saw Mila's glowing face on the screen.

"Speak of the devil," she said to Taina and then answered. "Hello?"

Taina silently signaled for her to put the phone on speaker so that she could hear the conversation. When Jay did, Taina heard Mila in the middle of saying, " . . . didn't call me when you got home. Neither did Taina."

"We're good," Jay said a little too fast. "In fact, I'm over here right now."

"Really?" Mila asked, sounding hurt. "And you didn't invite me?"

Taina rolled her eyes. Mila had been letting the pregnancy get to her, and lately, she'd been very sensitive. That was one of the biggest reasons Taina wanted their dwelling to remain a secret.

"You were so tired," Taina said. "You're always invited, but you need to rest, girl."

"OK, well then, here I come," said Mila.

"No!" Both Jay and Taina yelled in unison.

"What?"

"I-I mean . . ." Jay searched for a lie. "I'm not staying very long. I was just leaving."

"Uh-huh," Mila said. "You know what? You two bitches are acting weird, so I'm about to take my pregnant ass to sleep. Love y'all."

"Love you too," they said and disconnected the call.

"You think she knows we're lying?" Jay asked.

"Yup."

"You think she'll let it go?" Jay asked again.

"Nope."

Jay giggled, and Taina did too, for the first time since the Mario incident.

"Are you sure you're OK?"

Taina nodded.

"Yeah, I'm alive, right? I refuse to succumb to that self-loathing feeling again," Taina said and then got quiet. "You know he took my virginity in this hotel?"

"Seriously? Wow."

"Yeah," Taina said and thought back to that night. "I thought he was a really nice guy. I even snuck out the—"

Suddenly a lightbulb went off in her head. Jay noticed the wide-eyed blank stare and waved her hand in front of Taina's face.

"Earth to Taina."

"I know how we can get in."

Taina told her the rest of the story about how she snuck out that night, and Jay laughed excitedly.

"You're a fucking genius."

"Thanks, I like to think so myself."

The girls planned to sneak through the basement of the house. Taina was sure that the only people that would be roaming inside the place were the housekeepers.

"What if they aren't there?"

"They will be," Taina told her.

"Are you going to be able to do it?" Jay asked the question that had been hanging in the air. "Can kill your mother?"

"She tried to kill me," Taina answered.

"But will *you* be able to kill *her?*" Jay asked the question again. When Taina hesitated, Jay grabbed their room key. "Come on."

She had on her shoes and was out of the room before Taina could ask her where they were going. Taina hurried and threw some tennis shoes on and ran after her. To Taina's surprise, Jay took her up to the roof of the hotel.

"What do you see?" Jay asked once she felt Taina's presence behind her.

"Huh?" Taina panted, trying to catch her breath from all the stairs she'd just run up.

"Look down," Jay said, ignoring the chilly breeze hitting them. "What do you see? What do you smell?"

Taina put her hands in her hoodie and moved closer to the edge of the building.

"I see New York." Taina shrugged her shoulders. "I see people, and I smell . . . everything."

"What are those people doing?"

"Living their lives, I guess," Taina said.

"Exactly." Jay turned to Taina and stared at her deeply in the eyes. "They don't even know or care that girls like us exist. They don't give a *fuck,* Taina. They're living their life, just like you're trying to do. You're trying to live a life your mother has tried to take away from you *twice.* She doesn't care about you, especially if she puts a dollar on your head. She showed you no mercy. Mario didn't hurt you; your mother did. He was just following orders. So, now, what you gonna do about it?"

Taina's blood felt like it was boiling in her veins at the truth in Jay's words. That was *precisely* what Jay wanted.

"I'ma kill that bitch," Taina said. "Tomorrow at midnight, I'm going to kill her."

# Chapter 13

The next day, Jay called for someone to drop off one of their ABC company's vehicles to them. The two women checked out and proceeded to Taina's old neighborhood. It had been years since she'd seen any of the houses they passed. When Jay drove past Mrs. Sanchez's place, Taina remembered going there sometimes after school when she had soccer practice. They parked far enough from the gate to not be seen but close enough for their binoculars to reach. The whole day they monitored who entered and left.

It was almost ten p.m. when their targets finally pulled up at their home. Taina almost got out of the car when she saw her mother and Chris drive through the gates in a brand-new Audi. Later, they saw Isabella step out on one of the balconies upstairs with Chris. He was fondling her and kissing all over her body. All Taina could do was shake her head. Isabella was codependent. It made sense that she would fall into bed with the man who had taken Denny's place.

"Your moms is foul, yo," Jay said, shaking her head. "Not only is she fucking her deceased husband's cousin, but she done moved him up in the crib too. That ain't right."

Taina silently agreed with her friend. Her mother had banished her from a home that was rightfully hers and turned her back on her. Chris had always promised to protect her, but his greed was causing him to do just the opposite. Deep down, Taina knew that Chris might not have really forgiven her father for the mistake he'd made years ago, and at that moment, she regretted saving his life.

"Whoa," Jay said. "She a freak, though. They're fucking hard as shit on the balcony."

Taina gave Jay the side eye that said, *"Really, bitch?"*

Then Taina put her binoculars back to her eyes to look at the scene taking place. Jay was right. Chris was tearing up Isabella. Taina's heart wrenched with every delighted expression forming on her mother's face. She was disgusted. Isabella had the face of a woman with no problems, still looking young and carefree. At first glance, you would never be able to tell that she was the type of woman to put a $200,000 reward on her own daughter's head.

"Hopefully, this puts both of them to sleep," Taina said, looking at the clock in the minivan they were posted in. It read eleven thirty. "Almost showtime."

They began to load up, and as soon as the clock read eleven forty-five, they made a swift exit. Guns drawn, they ran with Taina covering the front and Jay in the back. Darkness cloaked them in the night. By the time they reached the gate, it was five minutes until midnight, and as Taina had said, the guard had already left his post.

"Do you remember the code?" Jay asked Taina, who nodded her reply.

She entered her father's month and date of birth, but the final numbers were the year she was born. The doors clanked open, and the two girls ran as fast as they could through them.

"To the back." Taina pointed at Jay to go toward the basement window.

Her body still ached, but her adrenaline was pumping so much that she barely felt the pain. They ducked and dodged the men patrolling the grounds until they finally reached the home stretch. Taina snatched Jay's arm and pulled her behind a bush. The two girls ducked, and Taina eyed the rotating camera.

"Damn," Jay panted. "Your dad must have been loaded."

"He owned a Fortune 500 company, and he also owned shares in two more. Oh, and he was a kingpin," Taina said.

"Yup, he was loaded."

Taina finally got the rotation right in her head and turned to Jay.

"I will go first because I know how to open the window. Don't look anywhere else but at me when I'm through, OK? You must run the exact moment I tell you to."

When Jay told Taina that she understood, Taina waited for the perfect moment and then took off running as fast as she could. It took her three seconds to get to the window and three more to push it open and slide through. She landed hard on her knees and fell to her side. Quickly, she rose to her feet and pointed her gun around the laundry room. Of course, it was empty. She pushed a crate to the wall under the window when she was sure the coast was clear. Standing on it, she waved and got Jay's attention.

"You have six seconds," she mouthed to Jay and did a countdown with three fingers while watching the camera. When the last finger came down, Jay took off running at the speed of an Olympic track star and slid through the window. Taina moved out of the way just in time, and Jay landed on her feet.

"OK," Jay said, dusting herself off. "The hard part is over."

"Follow me," Taina whispered. "Their room is this way."

Taina had been right again. The only people roaming the hallways were a few housekeepers, and staying out of their way wasn't too hard. Taina was taken back on memory lane when she smelled the scent of the house. Lavender. It had always been her mother's favorite fragrance. The girls tiptoed up the stairs until they reached Isabella's room. Their backs were to the wall, and they listened closely. They heard the shower running in the bathroom of the master bedroom. The location of one of their targets was known. Next, Taina heard the familiar sound of her laughter and knew that her mother was probably up watching reruns of *Friends*. Taina nodded her head to Jay. They had made both of their targets. Taina burst into the room, gun drawn, and flicked on the light switch.

Isabella gasped and tried to scream, but Jay was too quick for her. She slapped her so hard that she fell out of bed.

"Shut the fuck up," Jay hissed and jammed her gun in Isabella's face.

"Is it money you want?" Isabella's eyes were huge. She was terrified. "There's a safe in the closet. Take it all."

"Shut the fuck up," Jay whispered again.

That time, the blow she landed on Isabella's face drew blood. Although Isabella and Chris hadn't done anything personally to Jay, they may as well have. Taina was one of the most genuine people she had ever encountered in her life, and the fact that these people were trying to break her already broken soul pissed her off.

"Jay," Taina said. "The bathroom."

Taina nodded toward the bathroom, signaling Jay to grab Chris from the shower. She then turned her attention back to her mother, who still couldn't recognize her. Taina grabbed her by her hair and pulled her to the center of the large bedroom.

"W-who are you?" Isabella cried. "What do you want?"

"You to die," Taina said and removed her hood.

Isabella gasped, and if she had been terrified before, the feeling now tripled. She recognized her daughter instantly, but it was like staring into the face of a ghost. Taina was the last person she expected to see, and the sadness that had filled her eyes the time Isabella had last seen her was replaced with rage. Isabella knew Taina wasn't there to tell her how much she missed her.

"You are not welcome here," Isabella exclaimed.

"I kind of got that message when you never came to see me in the facility. I also got it when you wouldn't let me back to my home," Taina said, hitting her with the butt of her gun. "How can you be so cruel? You even sent someone to kill me."

"And clearly, the little ingrate that killed your father failed at it."

"You're my mother!" Taina kicked Isabella in her ribs. "Do you know what I've been through? When Marisol and Papi died, I didn't want to live anymore. I needed you, and you couldn't even love me. You *never* loved me."

"I never wanted to be a mother. But Denny wanted a child. Every time I looked at you, I saw the mistake I made." Isabelle shrugged despite the gun in her face. "You weren't my daughter. You were my burden, and you still are. If I had known I wouldn't have access to my money, I would have let you die when Stephanie found you overdosed."

Her words stung, and Taina bit back her tears. She didn't have a mother. She had a monster.

"I'm sorry I caused you so much discomfort, but that's over now. Goodbye, Isabella."

Isabella tried to lunge for the gun in Taina's hand, but it was too late. The gun went off, and the bullet caught her square in the forehead. Taina watched her fall to the ground and felt a single tear fall down her face. She was officially an orphan . . . a very rich one.

"Baby?"

Taina turned and saw Chris being brought from the bathroom, wearing only a pair of boxers. Jay's gun was on the back of his head.

He had seen Taina shoot his woman, and rage filled him like a helium balloon. He started to charge toward her, but two guns aimed at his head abruptly stopped him.

"Taina, what have you done?" Chris demanded, looking at Isabella's dead body. "Oh, no. What have you done?"

"I only did to her what you both were trying to do to me."

"Your father taught me long ago how easy it is to get rid of family when business calls for it. And business calls for it now. I should have known that bastard wouldn't be able to get the job done. I guess I'll have to do it myself."

"No, you won't. What you're going to do is step down. My father's fortune is mine. And so is his empire."

"Ha, little girl. You know nothing about running this business. They will eat you alive." The way he spoke, Taina barely recognized him.

She'd heard that money changed people, but she never thought that Chris would be one of those people. He laughed at the way she was looking at him.

"Cat got your tongue, little cousin?"

"What happened to you, Chris? You promised to protect me."

"Your biggest mistake was saving me that night," Chris told her. "Your second mistake was coming in here and forgetting that I, like your father, was raised on the battlefield."

Jay didn't know what hit her when Chris moved with the speed of a man two times younger than him. He grabbed her wrist and made her drop her weapon. Her arm was straight, and Chris hit her bone upward at the elbow.

"Aww!" Jay screamed when her bone cracked.

Taina tried to get a clear shot, but she didn't have one without hitting Jay first. Chris head-butted Jay, knocking her out cold, and then threw her into Taina. When Jay fell on the ground, Chris charged Taina.

"You made this easy for me, Taina," Chris said, grabbing her by her neck and kicking her gun away from her hand. "You came straight to me."

Chris spun her around and put her into a neck lock. Taina tried to say something to him, but she couldn't. Her hands flew to his muscular arms, and she clawed his arms. Her eyes fell on Jay, regretting that she had even let her join the mission. She reached for her friend's still body.

"I'm going to kill her," Chris whispered in her ears, and Taina felt the moistness from his breath. He squeezed a little harder, and she gasped, trying to get air, but her airway was completely shut.

"Right after I kill you. I never planned any of this to happen. You are my little cousin, and I loved you like a daughter, but you see, I have my own daughter now. She has your old room. I have responsibilities, and honestly, this is how Denny Capello can truly repay me for what he did to me all those years ago."

Everything around Taina began fading away, and she knew she was losing her grip on life. Her eyes shut, and she was about to succumb to death, until she heard Chris grunt in pain behind her and his grip on her loosened.

"Get off of her!"

Taina collapsed on her side and gasped for breath. Her throat felt like it was on fire, and she swallowed blood, but her lungs were happy to be filled once again. Taina rolled on her back and felt a gentle hand touch her face tenderly.

"Oh, Taina, I knew I heard your voice," Stephanie said, turning her back on Chris and kneeling beside Taina. "I thought you'd never come home."

In her hand, she was holding a bloody broken vase. Behind her, Taina saw Chris struggling back to his feet. Taina tried to warn Stephanie, but it was too late. Chris sent one of his fists crashing into the side of her face. He hit her a few more times before standing up straight. Taina looked around and saw that she was within arm's reach of the gun that Jay had dropped.

"I never liked that bitch," Chris grunted and went to finish off Taina.

"And the feeling is mutual," Taina said, holding the gun.

When Chris realized his mistake, he lunged at Taina just like Isabella had, but she was too quick for him. She shot him in his chest. Chris looked down at the wound with disbelief and gripped his chest. But instead of falling, he went after Taina once more, so she shot again. Then again . . . and again.

"Aaghhhh!" she yelled until she had emptied the entire magazine into his body.

Finally, Chris dropped to his knees, and blood gushed out of every bullet hole. He reached for Taina one last time before he fell forward on his face, dead. Taina kicked him for good measure. When she was sure he was dead, she dropped back down to the ground, barely able to hold herself up. She crawled over to Jay and gently shook her.

"Jay, please don't be dead," Taina said and then looked over her shoulder at Stephanie, who was groaning and holding her head.

"That son of a bitch hit me."

Taina was just happy that she was alive. She nudged Jay, and that time, she moved. Jay moaned and opened her eyes slowly. The first thing she saw was Taina's smiling face.

"Whoa," she said. "You don't look so good."

"Neither do you, bitch." Taina looked at Jay's arm and knew she needed medical attention.

She didn't have to wait long because before she knew it, the bedroom was invaded by men in suits. Their guns were drawn and pointed at everyone in the room. One of them recognized Taina instantly. Her resemblance to Denny was uncanny. He lowered his weapon and hurried to her side.

"Princess." He called her what all of Denny's soldiers called her, and she knew she was safe. "Are you OK? What happened?"

"Yes, I'm fine," Taina lied. "But my friend needs medical attention. Cousin Chris and my mother tried to kill us."

"You don't look fine," he said, softly touching her face. "I knew something wasn't right about her when she didn't bring you back home."

The man looked back at the others and used two fingers to point at Isabella and Chris's bodies. "Get them out of here. The rightful heir to the empire is home. Somebody call nine-one-one."

When the ambulances arrived, the men helped Stephanie, Taina, and Jay down the stairs to receive medical attention. Jay was put on a stretcher because of her arm, and Taina requested to ride with her. She didn't want them to be separated. She didn't hear the answer to her response because she suddenly heard a voice yelling at her. From where she was on the circular driveway in front of the house, Taina looked toward the gate, where she saw a very pregnant Mila and Frank waving at them, trying to get their attention.

"Tainaaaa!" Mila yelled. "Jay!"

Taina looked at her security and told them it was OK to let them through. Mila gave the man guarding the gate a dirty look.

"I told you I know her!" Mila huffed and moved fast for a pregnant woman until she reached the ambulance her friends were in. "I *knew* you were lying. I *knew* it. That's why I'm glad I put tracking on your cell phones."

Mila noticed Taina's bruised body and face, and then she saw Jay's broken arm. "What the fuck happened?"

"Let's just say,"—Taina grabbed Jay's hand and blew Stephanie a kiss before they shut the door to the ambulance she was in—"everyone who has ever wronged me got what they deserved."

Mila looked from Taina to Jay. "Let's just say that you both have me fucked up," she exclaimed and then got the paramedic's attention. "Umm, I will be riding in this ambulance with these women, and I believe they are ready to go. Just let me tell my fiancé to meet me at the hospital."

Frank, who had been standing behind her, had already heard everything. He kissed her on the cheek and helped her up the back of the truck so that she could sit next to her friends. The paramedic shut the door, and each girl sat on one of Jay's sides.

"Now, what happened?"

"Fuck that," Jay said, staring at Mila like she had laser vision. "When the fuck did you tap our phones?"

"Girl,"—Mila waved her hands—"I did that months ago. I don't know what I would do without you two. So last night, when you two were acting all weird and shit, I just kind of checked up on you and found out that you guys had lied to me. Why didn't you call me? I could have helped. But now look at you. Jay got a broken arm, and Taina's face is all fucked up. I can't believe you two."

"Calm down," Taina said soothingly. "You're going to upset my babies and go into early labor, and I really don't want to hear Frank's mouth."

"I'm cool, I'm cool," Mila said. "Now, tell me what happened."

"I'll tell you the whole story later. But for now, just know my mother turned out to be the Wicked Witch of the West. She hated me, and she showed me tonight."

"Wow, Taina," Mila said. "Your own mom?"

"Yeah," Taina said. "Crazy thing is I don't feel anything. The woman who saved our lives was more like a mother to me than my real mom. When I pulled the trigger, it felt like I was killing a total stranger."

Mila nodded her understanding.

"So . . . does that mean this is over? Once and for all?" Mila asked them and looked at Jay. "You don't have crazy assassins coming after you, do you? And, Taina, you don't have anybody else trying to steal your inheritance, right?"

Mila grabbed Jay's good hand and reached for one of Taina's. "While we were waiting outside of the gate, I heard gunshots. I didn't know what was happening, but I was scared I would lose you both. You two are my family now. Without you, I have no strength, love, or motivation."

"Somebody take the mic, please," Jay groaned, but Taina saw the tears welling up in her eyes.

"No, for real, Jay," Mila cried.

Taina knew how she felt. She had no family either, just them. Everybody else she had loved at one point was dead. The things they had gone through and the evils they'd witnessed were the glue that kept them bonded. In their friendship, you would find true love and loyalty, things families bonded by blood didn't always have.

"I know, Mila." Jay sniffled slightly. "I love you both too. Very much."

Taina kissed Jay on the forehead. "Thank you for being my ride or die tonight. For a moment there, I thought we were both dead."

"Yeah, I know. But you don't have to thank me," Jay said. "For you two, I'll ride to the end of the world and back."

"I mean, I would have been ride or die too if somebody would have picked up the phone and called me."

"We know," Taina and Jay said in unison, knowing that Mila would never let them live that night down.

They all broke into a fit of giggles, even though two of the girls were in pain. It seemed as though everything was right in the world finally. All three of them had lived and made it through hell. There were some things in life that they would never be able to get back and some dreadful memories that would always haunt them, but they would always have one another. To them, that was all that mattered. They were the epitome of true friendship; nothing would ever tear them apart. Jay squeezed Mila's hand, and Mila squeezed Taina's.

# Epilogue

The day was sunny when she made her way through the cemetery. It was the first time she'd ever been able to muster up enough courage to show her face at his grave since he'd been buried. It blew her mind that Denny still intimidated her even from the grave years later. His tombstone was a large angel, bigger than any of the others in the cemetery, and he was separated from the other deceased. It was a nice winter day, and the air was frigid, but that didn't stop Taina from making footprints in the snow to reach her father.

She breathed heavily when she finally reached where her father was laid to rest. She put her hand on the cold tombstone to wipe some snow away and read the engraved words:

*Here lies Denny Alexander Capello. A loved husband, father, and businessman. May he rest peacefully in the arms of forgiveness.*

"Hey, Papi," Taina said and kissed the tombstone. She felt a breeze on her cheek, and she smiled. "I know, I know. What took me so long, right? I'm sorry."

Taina knelt and talked like her father was kneeling right in front of her and in her face.

"I just wasn't ready to see you," she said. "It took me a while to come to terms with all of this. I never meant for you to die, Papi."

Taina took a deep breath. Everything in her life had finally fallen into place. Not only was she a part owner of ABC, but she also took control of all of her father's businesses, including the illegal part of it. She was doing good by Denny Capello's name and proved that she looked like him and had his hustle too. She moved out of her apartment and back into the house she'd grown up in. Jay visited often, and Mila brought the kids by whenever she could. But despite all her successes, she felt like something wasn't right in her life.

"Oh, Papi, I would do anything to have you here with me. I wish we could get another chance, but unfortunately, that's not how things can be. But I love you with all my heart."

Taina felt another breeze. That one seemed to linger on her cheek as if it were caressing it. A tear came to her eye, but she quickly wiped it away, remembering that her father hated to see her cry.

"Anyway, I have tons of news for you," she said. "I'm finally happy. I'll spare you the gory details of what has happened to me up until now. We all know how angry you get. I made two new friends. They're amazing. Mila is the nicest person that you'll ever meet. She sometimes has an attitude problem, but that's usually in the morning. She has twins now, so her nerves are really bad, but that's what tequila is for, right?"

Taina giggled a little bit.

"Her husband is my business partner. You should see how much work we're moving. We are about to close one of the biggest heroin and Ecstasy deals this state has ever seen. And Jay? She's a fighter. You would like her. Her loyalty speaks volumes. If I were to go against the world at this very minute, she would be right by my side. I won't tell you exactly what bonded us, but know that we are literally bonded by blood. I love them like my sisters, and I'm blessed to have them in my life. Stephanie is still around the house, fussing at me. She disagrees with me taking over parts of your business, but I'm a Capello. It's only right. I'll have to take a few months off, though, for the wedding and other things."

Taina smiled and pictured the surprised look she knew would have spread across her father's face.

"Yes, Papi," she said. "I met somebody. And no, he's not an undercover assassin. I did my research on this one. His name is Antonio, and he's a good guy. I love him very much. He loves me back and doesn't care about any of what happened in the past. He's giving me a fresh start. You would like him. He's smart and has a master's in accounting, so our finances look lovely if I say so myself."

Taina reached into her Alexander McQueen coat pocket and grabbed a wad of cash totaling $1,000.

"OK, Papi," she said, tucking the money inside one of the flower vases around his headstone. "That's enough for now. I would have brought you more flowers, but I thought you'd like this more. I'll come back next week. I love you. Oh, and I'm sorry for killing your wife."

She kissed his headstone and stood to her feet, holding the small of her back. There was one other person that she had come to see. She left her father's grave and took a few minutes to find another one. When she found it, she felt her heart skip a beat. There was also an angel on the gravestone, but it was small. She did just like she'd done with her father's tombstone and wiped away the snow.

*Here lies Marisol Ramos, beloved daughter, sister, and friend. When all hope seems lost, hope some more. Forgive and always put love out into the world because you only get what you give out.*

Taina sobbed because she could hear her best friend saying those exact words. Taina didn't care about the snow. She dropped to her knees and hugged the tombstone.

"Hi, Em," she whispered, letting her tears fall freely. "I miss you. I would tell you everything that's happened to me until now, but I think you already know. I feel horrible standing here alive while you're here buried. But knowing you, I know you're at peace. You were always the stronger one."

Taina shut her eyes and remembered Marisol's radiant smile and the hugs and kind words she gave Taina during tough times. Taina thought of Marisol daily. Whenever she thought of her, she couldn't believe she was gone.

"I kept your promise." Taina pulled away from the tombstone. "It may have taken me a while to get the courage to come here, but I never forgot about you. Not even once. I mean, who could? You were the best friend a person could hope to have. My new friends would have loved you. You would fit in perfectly just because we all love to laugh. I have some more news for you, though."

Taina smiled and heard Marisol's voice in her head saying, "Ooookay . . . I'm waiting."

"Well, I'm getting married to the love of my life," Taina said. "His name is Antonio, and I met him at a Super Bowl party last year. I know, I know. Crazy, right? But I followed your three rules this time around. Remember those? He loves me. The way he looks at me, I just know I'm safe. When I'm with him, it's like all the skeletons in my closet are nonexistent, you know? I hope heaven has tons of cute boys to keep you occupied." Taina giggled and put a hand to her stomach when she felt a flutter.

"That's not the only news I need to tell you. I didn't tell Papi yet, so please don't dry snitch up there, but I'm pregnant. Yes, girl, I promise I will love this baby until she gets sick of me."

Taina cradled her stomach. It had been five months since she found out she was pregnant, and she was just starting to get a little pregnancy pouch. She absolutely adored the little baby growing inside of her belly. Her love for it made it impossible to understand her mother's ill feelings toward her.

"It's a girl . . . I'm naming her Marisol. It just has a ring to it, don't you think?" Taina said and let her fingers gently brush against the tombstone. "I love you, girl, always and forever."

Taina said her goodbyes, promising to visit her whenever she came to visit Denny. Then she stood up and turned her back on them to go down to where her car was waiting. When she reached the vehicle, the back door opened.

"You OK?" Mila asked, stepping out of the Mercedes.

She took two steps to Taina and started fussing over her. She zipped up her coat for her and tightened her scarf. Ever since Mila found out that Taina was pregnant, it seemed she had turned into her own personal nurse.

"Yes, I feel so much better now." Taina smiled.

"Good." Mila smiled back.

"OK. We can go now. A bitch is hungry," Taina whined and walked to the passenger seat of the car.

Once her door and Mila's were shut, Jay locked them and looked at the two like they were crazy.

"Umm . . ." she said. "I have an unregistered weapon under my seat. I will need you two to put on your seat belts."

"Well, nobody told you to be riding around hot." Taina rolled her eyes but did as she was told.

"Well, nobody told you to be riding around hot," Jay mocked Taina. "I was just playing anyway. I'm not that stupid. Did you handle what you needed to handle?"

"Yes." Taina smiled. "Yes, I did."

"Good." Jay sounded genuinely relieved as she drove off. "Hopefully, now you won't be so uptight and bitchy. Little Marisol has you mean as hell."

"Fuck you," Taina said, surprised. "I am not mean. Huh, Mila?" She whipped her head around when she heard nothing but silence from the backseat. "Mila?"

Mila pretended to be looking out of the window, but when she saw Taina looking at her intensely, she burst out laughing.

"Dang. I was trying to sip my tea. But no, for real, Taina, you have been a *little* mean lately."

"I'm sorry, y'all. It's because I can't smoke my weed for another four months," Taina whined. "I'm all on edge and shit."

Everybody in the car laughed.

"I love you, for real," Taina said to her friend. "Both of you."

"Blood couldn't make us any closer." Jay nodded.

"Ride or die, fool. Ride or die," Mila said, sending them all into another fit of giggles.

Looking lovingly at one another, they said the one phrase that would bond them for eternity. Taina had never known a bond like that and was grateful that she could experience it for the rest of her life. She smiled at them and nodded.

*"Ride or die."*

# *The End*